RUNE BOUND

To Jenny
From Tina Jenkins

T.L. Jenkins

(c) BY T.L. JENKINS

COPYRIGHT 2013© COPYRIGHT HOLDER TINA L JENKINS, ALL RIGHTS RESERVED BY TINA L. JENKINS. DISTRIBUTED BY LULU.COM. ISBN 978-1-304-53269-5

To my loving husband, who inspired me to write a tale of Dwarves, and make it both an adventure, and a romance with a bit of quest mixed in.

TABLE OF CONTENTS

CHAPTER ONE	PAGE 1
CHAPTER TWO	PAGE 16
CHAPTER THREE	PAGE 30
CHAPTER FOUR	PAGE 38
CHAPTER FIVE	PAGE 47
CHAPTER SIX	PAGE 56
CHAPTER SEVEN	PAGE 67
CHAPTER EIGHT	PAGE 76
CHAPTER NINE	PAGE 85
CHAPTER TEN	PAGE 99
CHAPTER ELEVEN	PAGE 109
CHAPTER TWELVE	PAGE 120
CHAPTER THIRTEEN	PAGE 134
CHAPTER FOURTEEN	PAGE 143
CHAPTER FIFTEEN	PAGE 153
CHAPTER SIXTEEN	PAGE 163

CHAPTER ONE

Savanna gritted her teeth as she struggled to hold the wound while Gavan stitched the two pieces of flesh back together. The smell of blood and bile filled her nose, and she tried not to gag. All around her she could hear the moans of pain from the other wounded as they waited for their turn to get sewed up.

The tent of healing was so full the wounded now were being left outside in the pouring rain. This did not bode well for the wounded outside. The moisture would cause infection, and gangrene would put many at risk of loosing limbs or life.

The warrior that they were working on groaned as he started to come to, and Gavan swore in Dwarf as he stitched faster. His strong fingers pulling the blood slick needle through for the last stitch in the sword cut in the man's side. With deft fingers he tied the final knot just as the warrior opened his eyes. Then Gavan turned to the next patient leaving Savanna to finish up.

Savanna cleaned the blood from the warrior's body. She could feel the man's eyes upon her. She didn't like the looks he was giving her.

" Are you an angel?" The man croaked up at her.

Savanna shook her head in answer to his question. " Nay sir. I am just an assistant to doc here."

The man smiled, showing half rotted teeth. She shivered with something between disgust and fear.

She looked at Gavan across from her. He was already working on the next warrior, this one a fellow Dwarf in russet colored armor. She noticed the differences between the two Dwarves. Where Gavan was short, this one was tall and was broader in the shoulders. Otherwise they shared the same coloring. It was the medallions upon their chests that told her they were of the same bloodline.

Her heart lurched upon seeing them.

Secrets lay heavy upon her soul. Twin born on the hunter's moon didn't help either, or the fact that she to was part Dwarf. Only her twin brother knew the truth of their birth. But he had been killed a year after their mother had disclosed the truth on her deathbed.

" Your father doesn't know about you." She had told them. " We spent one night together. He went his way I went mine. Blasted Dwarf lied to me! Had you two Nine months later. Should have killed both of you at birth. Would have made my life easier." She never told them his name only he was Dwarf.

Savanna gritted her teeth at the memory, and at the pain it caused her. Half Dwarf and whatever her mother was, and working for Dwarves. She shook her head at the irony of it.

Her life would have turned out just like her mother's if some one hadn't been hunting her down to kill her. Thus it was, she never stayed in one spot for very long.

She had been fifteen when she had found her brothers body, mutilated and disfigured in the forest a year after their mother's death, words were written upon his bare chest ' your next Savanna' had frightened her so bad she had run, and was still running from the ones hunting her.

    She was always fearful that who ever they were would find her. What scared her the most was that they knew her name. When the war with Teirnan broke out, she found her chance of surviving by joining the company. Here she felt safe, and the attempts on her life had stopped.

    Something within her seemed to warn her when something bad was going to happen. That internal warning system had saved her life many times over the past few years. The last time it had been an arrow from the dark. She had no idea who wanted her dead, and she wasn't about to seek out the ones hunting her to find out.

    The man chuckled as his fingers found one of her stray strands of blond hair. " Maybe after your done here wench, you would like to find a quiet spot so we can get to know each other better."

    " Not in this life!"

    With a hiss, Savanna swept her hair from his fingers. Her dark eyes blazing, she left the man's side to join Gavan who was cutting the arrow shaft from the Dwarf's shoulder. The chuckle the man gave her departure made her blood boil in fury as he got up and left so his cot could be given to the next warrior.

    Gavan looked at her when she came to his side. He smirked, but didn't say anything about the man's

Proposal, after all he did warn her what would happen if she came with them. " It be on your head then. Don't expect me to keep the men off of you."

Those words had proved prophetic. Every human warrior in the company had either propositioned her, or told her to go home and raise some babies, and the Dwarves had told her that a woman didn't belong in a war campaign. She had heard it all.

Stubbornly she stayed and helped sew up the wounded. Two months of working non-stop next to Gavan, and still fighting for acceptance. Her temper keeping the men at bay with a sharp lash of words. Only once had she needed to use the dagger hidden on her thigh.

Savanna held her anger from her mission of cleaning the blood from the Dwarf. It wasn't his fault the man had made her angry, or that her life was so twisted. She shook as heat flowed into her at touching his flesh with her fingers. *I must be tired. If I don't get sleep soon I'm going to collapse, and Gavan's going to be angry that I didn't tell him how tired I truly am.*

It was the slight tightening of his muscles that told her she was hurting him. Contrite, she whispered. " Sorry."

She was so exhausted her hands shook, and she tried to hide it from the Dwarves, but they both noticed, and Savanna struggled not to cry.

She would not cry in front of them, especially

in front of Gavan. All her tears would do is give them more ammo to use to get her to go home, only she had no home to go to. She would save her tears for when she was inside her tent.

Gavan pulled the arrow out with a sickening pop. He let it fall to the ground as he then cleaned the wound as fresh blood flowed from the slit the arrow had left. He slathered his greenish white ointment liberally into the wound before reaching for the needle that Savanna held out to him.

Savanna handed him the needle already threaded and ready to be used with her other hand as she gently wiped the blood from the Dwarf's shoulder. His eyes watching every thing she did with interest as he held his red chain mail out of their way while they worked on his wound. Once more heat laced through her and her belly tightened. *Gods what is wrong with me? I never felt this with the other wounded!*

Thankfully she and Gavan weren't the only healers here, or they would be over worked. Already she could feel how tired she was. Her eyes burned from lack of sleep, and her head hurt from straining to see into each wound.

Her gift to heal she had kept from every one. Not even Gavan knew she could heal with her mind. All this time she had been burning out any infection she found. She could have healed all of the wounds herself, but then she would have a lot of explaining to do.

So she had learned to control her power to the minute amount to burn the infection from the Dwarf's wound while Gavan stitched, unaware of what she did. She had learned this trick in the last year while healing among the villages she had traveled through before joining the Thirteenth Company.

Gavan pulled the needle through and knotted it. With a snip of his scissors, he then put a clean bandage on the wound. The wounded Dwarf said something to him in Dwarf. Who chuckled and answered in the same way.

Then they looked at her. Which made her nervous when they both chuckled. Once again Savanna wished she could speak Dwarf. She hated not knowing what they said around her. Especially seeing as this company was made of one thousand Dwarves and One hundred humans and her, minus the six they lost in battle that morning. An all male Company with her the only female didn't bode well in any eyes, and many eyes of the stray warriors they had come across had been knowing, and the word Doxy had been whispered behind her back with speculative grins and propositions.

Savanna blushed as her eyes met the wounded ones eyes. They smoldered into her making her belly clench with swirling heat. She swayed and would have fallen if Gavan hadn't steadied her with a firm hand.

" Go get some rest." Gavan told her. " Your too tired to be of any use tonight. No arguing, just go."

At that moment the night healers came into the tent. They all nodded to Gavan, but ignored her completely.

Savanna sighed and put the cloth into her now blood filled bucket. She picked the bucket up and headed for the back entrance. She kept the hurt from her eyes as she passed the other healers.

They didn't approve of her helping in the tent of healing. The last skirmish with the enemy had left twenty wounded and six dead. Only one Dwarf had fallen in that battle. She had helped heal fifteen of those wounded. Some she had to help as Gavan held a leg or arm as she cauterized the weeping wounds with a hot poker that was kept hot in the brazier by the entrance. Tears had stung her eyes from both their screams of pain, and from the smell of burning flesh.

So tired was she that she didn't notice that the Dwarf who they had just stitched up was following her. The rain had stopped, and the moon had come out from behind the clouds.

The air was chilly, and she wasn't looking forward to sleeping in her tent. She hoped her dress was dry so she could wear it in the morning.

A chill breeze made her shiver with cold. It was going to be even colder in her tent. The company failed to provide her with a brazier and a cot, so her blankets lay on the cold hard ground inside her tent. At least they did give her a tent to sleep in even if it lay outside the encampment.

Argon Pass lay two miles south of the

encampment. Hard terrain lay between them, and the armed forces that held the Teirnan army at bay. The only way to get to the encampment was through that pass, but the Dwarves and there allied humans held it with iron fists. Only the wounded were shipped back so they could be healed enough to once more join the front lines.

    It wasn't until she dumped the bucket and turned to go to the pool to clean up that she finally noticed him. Surprised, she stopped and looked at him. " May I help you?"

    " You are Savanna." His voice was deep, and sent shivers of heat through her. It was more of a statement than a question. She liked his voice. Even his heavy accent gave him an exoticness that intrigued her and made her belly quiver strangely.

    " Yes." Savanna tensed. She didn't like the way his dark eyes roved over her and then stop at her cleavage, or the way her breasts tingled in answer to his look. He was a head taller than she, and he was wide enough to swallow her in his embrace if he was so inclined to hug her. Her mouth went dry at the thought, and fear, and something else swept through her. He could hurt her quite easily with his strength even injured as he was, and at the same time a tiny voice inside her wondered what it would be like to have him wrap her into his arms, and press her into his very wide chest. Her fingers tingled to wrap themselves into his long black beard. ***Damn, what the hell is wrong with me!***

He smiled. " My name is Oran. I just wanted to thank you for your help, and for your healing of my company.

Savanna was shocked as she realized whom she had helped heal. She now knew whom this russet armored Dwarf was. Lord Oran was the commander of the whole company. She had never met him until now, for he had been out in the battlefield for the last two months.

The urge to kill Gavan swept through her. He had known whom this Dwarf was and had kept that knowledge from her on purpose. Her belly tightened even more, making her head swim.

" Thanks are not necessary sir. Its my duty to help where I can sir." She told him. Her eyes stared at the ground. The flush of heat to her face told her she was blushing. The memory of his gaze stopping at her cleavage made her look at her chest. She groaned in dismay at the blood that covered her dress from top to bottom. She looked like she had been swimming in a pool of it.

Savanna swallowed the bile that rose into her throat. She would not vomit in front of Lord Oran. Bad enough she didn't know his identity only to vomit her last meal all over his boots even if that meal happened to be her breakfast. Her stomach tightened with hunger, or tension she didn't know. **Please gods don't let my night get any worse!**

He told her with a chuckle. " My brother Gavan speaks highly of you."

"Gavan is your brother?" Savanna looked up at him in shocked surprise. She really was going to kill Gavin when she saw him in the morning. She swallowed the groan of dismay that rose within her.

Lord Oran smiled, " He never told you. Well he may have his reasons, what they are." He shrugged his shoulders only to wince as his wound protested the action.

" Don't you dare go tearing those stitches out!" Savanna snapped and put her hand on his shoulder to check for bleeding. She had just put her hands on the bandage when she felt power fill her. With a gasp she tried to hold it back but she was too tired to stop it. Uncontrolled it flowed from her fingers into the wound. Wild power and heat so hot swept through her making her throw back her head and scream, but no sound came out.

Oran felt a hot jolt of lightning from her touch. In shock he looked at the small woman before him with new eyes. Her head was flung back and her mouth open in a silent cry. Onyx eyes blazed with power. Then it was gone as suddenly as it appeared, and he caught her just as she fainted.

With a growl Oran looked into the girls face. He was surprised by how light she was and how good she felt in his arms. Holding her tightly to his chest he carried her through the camp to his tent, hoping no one saw them. This girl had a lot of explaining to do when she came to.

He entered his tent and placed her upon the cot. She looked like a small child upon his covers and was surprised when his heart lurched to see her there. He took in her coloring and bone structure. Hair so blond it was almost white, an oval face with an olive like complexion. There was something familiar about her that he couldn't put his finger on that made his heart lurch again painfully.

One of his men, probably Braun, had set up his bath. Steam still rose from the clean water. He looked at the girl covered in blood on his covers and groaned. His body craved to be clean, but the girl needed to be cleaned as well. Her once light blue dress was soaked in blood and blood was smeared on one cheek and across her forehead.

Oran removed his bandage to check his wound. Since the girl had touched him his wound had stopped hurting. What met his startled eyes was whole flesh, even the stitches that Gavan had put in were gone. Not even a scar or red mark to show where the wound had been. The girl had healed him. ***Who is she and why do I feel like I should know her?***

The sound of feet outside his tent warned him that he was about to have company. With a growl, he turned and went to see whom it was.

Braun stood before him in his black and silver leathers and black armor his silver chain winking in the lantern hanging at his side from one hand. His eyes alert and filled with mischief. " Saw you heading to your tent with a pretty baggage in arms. Need some help?"

Oran thought swiftly and made a decision. Here was an answer to his problem and he knew Braun could keep his mouth shut. " As a matter of fact you can. I will need you to go to the girl's tent and bring a clean set of clothes for her. Then you can stand watch outside my tent and keep others from entering and the girl from leaving."

Braun raised one brow then chuckled, " Sure. Anything else?"

Oran sighed, " Some food for the two of us would be appreciated. The girl has been working since before sunup and has collapsed from exhaustion."

Braun's face darkened with concern. " Is she going to be alright? I know some of the men have been hard on her. She has more backbone than some of the humans in our company. She's a feisty little thing. Not afraid to say what's on her mind either," Then chuckled wickedly as his eyes sparkled with humor. " Fast with a knife to."

Oran was surprised. " So you approve of her being with the company?"

Braun snorted. " She has worked hard in the tent of healing, and has stood up to adversity with the men. For me, she has earned the right to be here." Then chuckled. " More than some humans that I know."

Oran's eyes widened in surprise at his friends words. For him to say what he had about Savanna, had been an eye opener on the character of the girl. It gave him food for thought. *But that still doesn't tell me who she is?*

" Go." He told Braun. " She will be spending the night in my tent for now." As an after thought he said, "And send Gavan here to look her over."

And maybe he can tell me more Oran thought Gavan's been working with her, he must know something about her.

Braun headed to the girls tent that lay just on the outskirts of the encampment with the lantern swinging at his side. He passed fires where Dwarves and humans laughed or sang or stared silently into flames depending on the mood of each group. None paid any attention to him once they recognized him as he passed only a nod from one or two Dwarves dressed in russet. Without hesitation he entered her tent and stood in shock at the sparseness of the interior. *She sleeps on the ground? What happened to her cot?*

Braun's eyes widened when he saw a dress hanging from a rope that she had strung across the far side of the tent. He could see water still dripping from the hem to land in the small lake that had formed under it in the lantern light he could see that lake soaking into her bedding. *She was going to sleep in this? Even prisoners had better quarters! No brazier either!*

Pity filled him along with anger. *I knew they were hard on her, but this?* Now guilt filled him *I should have checked on her before leaving with*

Oran. To be living in this for two months?

Shaking his head he left to find the supply wagons. *I'll deal with this later..*

He guessed the girls age to be in her late teens early twenties and a tiny thing no taller than five foot.

Reaching the wagons with the supply of clothes and other necessities, he heard them singing a ballad before he saw the fire where the supply Men was gathered. Eight men looked up at his arrival. The song ended and the chief of supply stood and went to him.

" What can I do for you my Lord Braun?" The man asked as he towered over the Dwarf in gray leathers. His six foot six heavy set frame making the Dwarf's five foot four seem more like a child's height but the Dwarf's frame was thicker.

" I need access to your wagons." Braun told him. " I need breaches and a shirt."

The man nodded and headed to the closest wagon. He pulled open the flap and looked into a crate. " What size?"

" Small." Braun told him.

The supply chief gave him a strange look then shrugged his shoulders and brought out the items asked for and handing him black leather breaches and a white shirt. " Anything else you be needing tonight?"

Braun shook his shaggy head at him. " No this is all that's needed for the moment. Thank you Chief."

Braun found the healer's tent and called gruffly, " Gavan?"

" What?" came the muffled reply from with-in.
"Savanna collapsed" Braun answered. " Oran has her in his tent."

CHAPTER TWO

Oran re-entered his tent as soon as Braun turned to leave. He looked once more upon the sleeping girl. She can wait for her bath when she wakes. Right now his body crawled with the need to bathe. He quickly stripped out of his russet armor and filthy garments and climbed into the tub.

He leaned back into the water with a sigh of pleasure. The heat from the water was swiftly killing the chill from his bones, and the soreness from his muscles. Taking the sponge and the bar of soap he rubbed the two together to get a good lather going. Vigorously he scrubbed his body with the soap-covered sponge. It didn't take the water long to go black with dirt and old blood. His long hair and beard held the most of it. They always did. Once he felt clean he stepped out of the tub and took the bath towel and rubbed the moisture from his body.

Oran put on his night pants but left the shirt off. He was too warm from both the bath and the blazing fire from the brazier. Taking up his axe he proceeded to clean it of the grime accumulated from battle.

He loved his axe. It had been his birthing gift from his father when he had come of age. It still looked the same as the day he had gotten it though it had seen many battles since. The metal was unflawed and bright in the firelight. Dwarven runes etched the metal and ran up into the handle. Once again he read them as he cleaned it ' δαρκ χλεαϖερ' Dark Cleaver.

He smiled as he finished cleaning his axe. With a sigh he put it upon its stand at the foot of his cot. His eyes once more looked at the filthy girl on the cot and he grimaced when she sighed and rolled over smearing blood on his covers. They would have to be changed before he climbed in them. The girl's skin had more color now that she had been resting, but she still slept soundly. She probably won't wake till close to morning.

Oran ran his fingers over the flesh she had healed. She mystified him. **She looks human, but the power that flowed from her says otherwise. Who is she? Who are her people? Why is she alone without any guidance?** It didn't make any sense to him at all. *Those gifted such as she are cherished and protected. Who has cast her out and why?*

A grunt from outside told him that he had company. Going to the entrance he looked out to find Gavan standing there with a face like stone and dark eyes gleaming with anger and concern. He had changed into his russet leathers minus the red chain mail. Beard and hair still wet from a recent bath. He also held a fresh set of clothing in his arms.

" The girls sleeping." Oran told him as he gave his brother room to enter the tent.

Gavan took no time to enter and go to the cot where the girl lay handing the clothing to Oran as he passed. He checked her over then leaned back on his heals with a grunt. " Total exhaustion. She needs a days rest."

Oran nodded as he placed the clothing on one of the chairs next to the table. He touched the place she had healed then said, " What do you know of this girl?"

" Not much. Why?" Gavan turned and looked at him quizzically. Then his eyes looked at the flesh he had just stitched and gasped as he stood up and went to take a closer look.

" I remember stitching this." He ran his fingers over the flesh in wonder.

Oran looked at the girl on the cot. " Did you know she could heal?"

Gavan was startled. " She did this? Savanna?"

Oran nodded as his brother's eyes widened in disbelief. He could see that Gavan was just as surprised as he was.

Gavan shook his head in wonder. He pursed his lips in thought. *The day I met the girl she had been helping in the town with some of the wounded humans. It was then that she had come to me for a job with the Company. I never understood why. She has been closed mouth about her past but was insistent on going with us.*

" Is she going to wake up soon?" Oran asked. " I really would like my bed back and she needs to bathe."

Oran groaned as the girl rolled onto her stomach spreading more blood over his bedding. He was going to need clean coverings by the time she got through with his bed.

Gavan snickered. He found the situation hilarious. Though the problem of the girl still hung heavy inside the tent. *At least it wasn't my covers that were being mucked up with blood.*

" Oran?" Braun called from the entrance. " Got a tray of food for you and the girl if she's awake."

Glad of the diversion, Oran went to the entrance and held the flap open so Braun could enter. He watched as his friend put the tray on the table. Then watched as his eyes widened in shock as he saw his shoulder where his wound had been.

" I saw the arrow that hit you." Braun reached out and touched the spot where the arrow had gone in with wondering fingers. His fingers shook as he touched the unmarked flesh. " How?"

" The girl." Both brothers growled in unison.

Braun's eyes widened as he looked with surprise upon the sleeping girl on the now mucked up cot. " Her?!"

It was too much, Braun burst out laughing. He laughed even harder at the chagrined looks the two brothers threw at him. Tears rolled down his face and disappear into his long beard as he doubled over clutching his belly.

Gavan sighed as their childhood friend laughed at them. Yes they deserved it. They had seen only a human girl trying to fit in with Dwarves and had gone no further into whom she really was. Especially as he had been working with her all this time and hadn't even guessed that she could be gifted. His fathers words came into his mind, " Never judge anything by its packaging for you may be surprised at the treasure that may lay within."

Oran growled. " Okay. We need to deal with this child. I would like to have my bed back and the girl really needs a bath."

Gavan heard the exhaustion in his voice and sighed as he once more looked at the girl. Yes, she did need a bath but she wasn't going to wake to do it herself. There was only one solution to that part of the problem. He looked at his brother as humor made him chuckle. His brother wasn't going to like this but if he wanted his bed back he saw no choice.

" We are going to bathe her." Gavan told them.

" Ah, Hell No!" Oran almost shouted.

" Are you crazy?" Braun snarled.

Gavan looked at Oran with amusement on his face. " You want your bed back?"

Oran turned red, " Can't you just wake the girl?"

Gavan smiled at his brother, " No."

Oran looked like he was going to hit something. Gavan only chuckled as he watched the myriad of emotions that swept through his face. ***This is just too delicious.***

With a low growl Oran grudgingly agreed. He helped Gavan as they got the girl out of her bloody dress. Oran's eyes widened when he found the knife strapped to her thigh. ***Braun said she had a knife***.

Unbuckling it Oran unsheathed it and looked at the dagger now in his hand then at the girl in surprise. ***She's fast with this? This is more like a double-edged dagger than a knife!***

Oran ran an appreciative eye over the blade. ***This is well made. Looks to be a mix of steal and silver.*** His finger touched the stone at the top of the hilt and he breathed in wonder. ***Onyx and unflawed! This stone alone is worth a fortune! Why a metal smith would put a stone like this into a hilt of any weapon doesn't make any sense. How did this girl come to be in possession of it?***

Oran placed the weapon back into its sheath and placed it gently onto the stand with his axe.

Gavan had placed the girl into the tub. The water was tepid but it would do to get the girl clean.

Braun stripped the bed and with the bloody mess along with the girls dress in his arms left to exchange them for clean ones. Leaving the two brothers with the job of bathing Savanna who was blissfully unaware of the process.

Gavan washed her hair while Oran took up the soap-lathered sponge to wash her front.

Gavan had just lifted her hair up to wash her neck when he stopped. His fingers touched the mark that lay before his eyes. She bore the birthmark of the Dwarves.

Oran tried not looking at what he sponged but he couldn't stop the flush that suffused his face or the tightening in his loins when he reached her breasts then her area between her legs. He heard his brother grunt and looked to see what had surprised him.

Gavan looked up at him with shocked eyes. " She's Dwarf."

In disbelief Oran leaned over to look at the silver ringed birthmark Gavan pointed to. His eyes widened then narrowed. He looked closely at the girls features and coloring. " Not fully."

Gavan snorted. " She's of the blood Oran. You know we can't breed with humans. How this child came to be outside our holdings needs to be answered as well as who birthed her."

Oran grimly nodded. His brother was right. The mystery surrounding this girl only grew deeper. ***Who was she and who was the girl's mother? That a woman outside the Holt had gotten with child from a Dwarf is a miracle.***

Braun returned with fresh bedding. He made the bed while the now silent brothers dried the girl with towels. They got her dressed in the shirt and breaches when he finished. To his surprise he watched as Gavan pulled the covers back and Oran placed the girl back into the cot. He gave them a look of query when Gavan gently brushed her hair from her face.

Oran motioned for them all to sit at the table. His exhaustion was forgotten. He went to his cupboard and pulled out his bottle of spiced rum and three glasses.

Gavan took a glass filled with the dark liquid and downed it in one shot. It helped warm the spot inside him that had grown chilled when he found the mark.

Oran did the same. His face was darker with speculation than it had been when Braun left.

Braun took his glass but didn't drink. He watched his friends waiting for them to speak. Worry lined the corners of his eyes. Something had disturbed his friends.

Oran looked at Gavan. " Has she spoken to you about her family at all?"

Gavan shook his head. " No. She told me she has no family. She's alone."

Braun was mystified but waited.

" Hell Oran she's of the blood!" Gavan growled taking another shot of rum. " Who fathered her Oran?"

Oran shook his head. His eyes strayed to the girl on the cot with contemplation in their depths.

Braun stiffened as shock swept through him as he turned to look at the sleeping girl. *If she is of the blood, then through the blood the truth can be known. Not all Dwarves know this. I know because my mother is a blood mage. She could read the blood of those around her. Knew the bloodlines and all connected to those lines. I can read the blood as well, but I have to taste the blood of the one in question to tell whose line they belonged to. Mother can see the lines with her eyes and with a touch. This will also link the girl to me.* Braun shivered in dread as he looked at her. *I will always feel this girl's emotions but if that's the price I must pay for giving truth to my friends then so be it.*

" I can find out." Braun grimaced. " But its not going to be easy."

Both of them looked at him in surprise.

Braun grimaced. " Through her blood I can see whose line she comes from. The only problem is that I may become lost within it. Its dangerous but what choice do you have. You need answers and I can give you those answers tonight."

The brothers looked at each other. They contemplated his words then both looked at him and nodded.

" What ever happens you mustn't touch me." Braun warned them. He tried to stress the seriousness to them if they did try to touch him while he was reading her blood. " It could kill me."

Grimly they both nodded. They would do as he asked and leave him be.

Going to the girl, Braun took out his knife and closing his eyes he took a deep breath, mumbled under his breath then gently poked her index finger with the knifes tip. He sat cross-legged on the floor next to the cot, then licked the small drop of blood from the tip. As he waited for the blood to open for him he saw the small wound on the girls finger heal up right before his eyes. He laid the knife on the floor in front of him. That was when the blood opened and took him by surprise at the power he felt from that small dose. *So much power!*

Instantly he was swept into it. The room vanished and her life story came alive within his mind. He saw the womb that held her and her twin. Emotion swirled through him at the realization that she was twin born. He saw the Hunter's moon shinning over the twins as they were born.

Where's her twin? Even as he thought that, the blood showed him her twin's death. His final moments as the dark hooded figure took his life. Sadness filled him.

Who's her mother? Darkness swirled through him. He saw a mountain dark and forbidding fill his mind. Teirnan. A woman was riding swiftly away from that mountain. She was angry and very upset. He could see that she was weeping.

The darkness swirled again. He saw a hut nestled against a mountain pass. The same woman was in a garden kneeling among some herbs. Her hand glowed with a green light and the plant started to grow. Her mouth moved as if she was talking to the plant. She looked up and stared at the forest. Anger and fear flitted across her face and a hooded figure stood just inside the forest watching her. Words hissed from her mouth full of power and the figure screamed in rage as it disappeared.

Once again the darkness swept him to another time and place. Now he was standing in a small tent. The scene made him stiffen for here was the night of passion that had brought forth Savanna and her twin. The woman from the mountain was ridding the Dwarf and her white hair covered the Dwarf's face from view. No matter how hard he tried he couldn't see his face. The darkness swirled around him to his frustration.

Who is Savanna's father?!

    Oran and Gavan sat quietly at the table. They talked of meaningless things as they watched their friend. They had almost finished the bottle of rum that sat between them and had picked at the food.

    Gavan swirled the contents of his glass slowly. He watched the motion of the rum with troubled eyes. He wanted to go to Braun and end this, but Braun's words stopped him. All three of them had been childhood friends. They had done almost every thing together including getting into trouble.

    Oran also swirled his glass of rum but his eyes were on the Dwarf on the floor. " How long has it been?"

    Gavan looked at the candle and sighed, " Just over a full mark."

    " How come he never told us he had this gift?" Oran sighed looking at his brother with hurt eyes. " Did he feel we would treat him any differently? I just don't understand. Hell, he's my friend!"

    Gavan raised a brow at his outburst. " He's my friend too Oran and he never told me. Never even hinted about his gift."

    " I'm not going to take this much longer." Oran growled low in his throat. " If he doesn't come out soon I'm going to loose my sanity."

The Dwarf on the floor moaned as if in pain and both brothers stiffened but didn't go to him. Their eyes completely glued to their friend. Worry lined their faces. They prayed he would come out of this unharmed.

Braun fought the swirling darkness. Seeking the truth now of the girl's father but the darkness continued to swirl. Angry he roared *'Who's her Father?!'* More demand than question. The darkness vanished with a physical pop! The jolt it gave him burned painfully through every nerve ending in his body. His mind filled with the image of a Dwarf. *No!* His mind tried to shy from that image but the blood showed him the girl's father. The image made him scream in denial. Into his mind came the image of his own father. Blood called to blood! Brother to sister! ***NOOOOO!***

" No!!" Braun croaked as his eyes snapped open to look at the girl on the cot in horror. " No!"

Oran reached him first. Concern darkened his face as he tried to steady him as Braun tried to stand.

Braun had broken into a cold sweat. Anguish filling his face and eyes. All he could do was breath hoarsely as his eyes were glued to the sleeping girl. ***She's my sister! Twin born! Conceived the same year father was killed! How could father betray mother like this?***

Gavan took his face and forced him to look into his eyes. Satisfied he let Braun go. " Shock. A good nights sleep and you'll be fine."

Braun looked at them in horror. ***Fine? I will never be fine after this!*** He tried to speak but his mouth was dry and wouldn't work. A glass was put into his hand and he downed the contents with a gulp. Hot-spiced rum blasted through the ice that seemed to be his blood. He shook violently in reaction. Her blood still filled his mind with images.

He finally croaked out " She's my half sister."

" What?!" Oran's eyes widened in disbelief at what his friend told them.

Gavan stiffened. He now understood the look of horror his friend had been sporting. Sympathy swelled within him for his friend. What Braun told them next made them both curse in Dwarf.

" Her mother comes from Teirnan. She's a Mage." Braun looked at them with haunted eyes. ***How can this be? Is she a mage as well?***

" Well." Gavan growled as he looked down at the sleeping girl. His voice was grim.

" So what would you have us do with her?" He asked Braun. His eyes dark and held no emotion at all. After all they were at war with the mages of Teirnan. ***Could she be a spy sent to infiltrate our defenses?***

" Do you think she could be a spy?" Oran growled as if he had read his mind. His hand instinctively reached for his axe but his fingers found only empty space for it wasn't at his girth but on its stand across the tent with the girl's dagger.

Braun shook his head. " She doesn't know what she is. Her mother never told her. Both mother and towns folk had treated her and her twin like they were cursed. She has been hiding for two years among the humans who never saw more than we did. A human child." Then he added, " Oran she'll be eighteen on the hunters moon month and a half from now."

Mages come into their full power on the night of their eighteenth year…

" Still I don't trust her." Oran growled. He went to his chest and pulled out a rope.

" So you mean to bind her?" Gavan barked in anger. His eyes blazed at Oran.

Braun was silent for the girls blood swept him further into the girl's life unaware that Oran was binding her.

CHAPTER THREE

Savanna woke to voices, Dwarven voices that were talking gruffly inside her tent. Startled by that she opened her eyes and looked for the ones talking. Her eyes fell on three Dwarves standing around her one in russet leather was Gavan, Oran in white night pants and a black and silver armored Dwarf she had never met. She realized that this wasn't her tent at all for she was on a cot. Then memory of what she had done filled her confused mind. Fear clutched her heart and she felt her face pale. *I healed Lord Oran! Are they going to punish me? Are they going to throw me out for keeping my gift from them? Will they curse me and try to kill me like the villagers?*

Her heart fell when she saw their faces like stone and eyes just as hard. She went to move but found her-self tied to the bed with ropes. Panic filled her. *They're going to hurt me!*

Sobbing in terror Savanna fought the ropes. Her flesh burned as she twisted her wrists trying to pull her hands from the ropes that bound her. Tears rolled down her face. She couldn't get free!

She screamed in fear as Lord Oran came towards her. His anger blazed from his hard eyes. Shivering in fright she stammered, " Are you going to kill me?"

Gavan growled. " It depends on you."

" Whom do you work for?" Lord Oran snarled mere inches from her face. Causing her to sink as far into the cot as she could. Her body shuddered uncontrollably. The smell of rum clung heavily upon him.

Savanna was so frightened she could only sob and gasp. Her throat had tightened and all she could do was stare into his blazing eyes in confusion. ***Work for? What did he mean by that? I work for Gavan.*** " G..Gavan."

Lord Oran sneered cruelly into her frightened face.

" You lie!" He snarled fists clenched as if to strike her.

" Who is your Teirnan master!"

Savanna whimpered in terror. ***They think I'm a mage!*** Her stomach roiled within her and she twisted just as vomit spewed from her mouth to soak the covers. The smell of her bile made her cry uncontrollably. ***They're going to kill me!***

Her mind screamed and like a cornered animal she started to fight. All her instincts screamed for escape. Heat consumed her blood and she saw red. Her internal warning system kicked into overdrive every nerve ending screamed ***'RUN!'***

Lord Oran's large hand tried to cover her mouth and she twisted with a snarl and bit down hard. The salty bitterness of blood ran over her tongue and swallowed convulsively as it flowed down her throat as she growled in rage and fear. She heard a roaring in her ears as something hard hit her on the side of the face.

His fist.

It hurt but still she fought.

Pain as he grabbed her hair, which made her cry out not from the pain but from desire that filled her blood with molten heat releasing the hand. Like an animal she snarled and thrashed trying to get free. Her need to fight warred with the need to cling to this male making her scream in denial. ***No!***

Then suddenly she was free! With a scream of rage and fear and full arousal she clawed his face with both hands. Her chest heaved trying to throw him off backfired as pleasure and molten heat slammed into her. But he only growled in answer and held her down with his body shocking her with his weight and sending a blast of heat through her body. His other hand grabbed one then the other of her wrists confining her again. His beard brushed her face and neck making her skin tingle even more as his breath heated her skin. His knees were between her legs sending intense heat through her lower body. She saw the intent in his blazing eyes as his hips and swollen member ground into her. Realization swept through her. ***He's going to rape me!*** Duel emotions screamed within her. ***Yes! No! Pain!?***

Her mind recoiled in shock at the duel emotions warring inside her and in pain her stomach roiled again and gurgling she twisted violently as vomit once more spewed forth from her mouth. As the vomit left her body so to did her strength. She lay weeping under him her body hot and tingling and hurting. ***No! This***

can't be happening! I can't want this male!

" Kill me then and have done with it." She snapped her eyes blazing. Too exhausted to fight. She snarled through her tears. " My mother was right, she should have killed me at birth."

Tears rolled down her hot cheeks. Her body trembled beneath his.

Lord Oran still griped her hands with one hand and let her hair go with the other. She waited for him to strangle the life from her. At least this way she knew who had killed her and not some phantom arrow from the dark.

Her eyes widened when all he did was reach down and start fumbling with his night pants. His face was inches from her and he was growling down at her with blazing eyes. Her blood turned to ice within her.

" Oran?" Gavan chocked from somewhere behind them. " Oran don't!"

Savanna felt him stiffen and look behind him then he swore in Dwarf. He snarled curses into her face then released her and got up. She looked at them through the ice that seemed to be consuming her from the inside.

He was looking at Gavan who was holding back the other Dwarf with all his strength who was snarling and weeping trying to reach him.

Savanna took advantage of the fact that none of them were looking at her to roll weekly from the cot. Her left side of her face ached where he had hit her and her hair was covered in her own vomit made her stomach roil again and once again bile rose in her throat, it spewed from her mouth to land on the ground before her. Her body shook with exhaustion and dry heaves as her belly had nothing left to expel. Tears still rolled down her face. She slowly crawled to the corner of the tent as far from the cot as she could. The exit too far for her in the state she was in. She curled up against the tent's wall shivering from the cold that was radiating through her.

    Savanna watched as Lord Oran and Gavan started to talk to the other in Dwarf. She couldn't stop shivering. Even her teeth had started to chatter loudly even to her ears. Her eyes glued to the three Dwarves standing a couple feet from her blocking the exit with their large bodies. She saw the strange Dwarf shudder then suddenly fall to his knees weeping hoarsely. ***He weeps for me! Why?***

    Gavan let him go and Savanna watched with wide eyes as the weeping Dwarf crawled towards her. She whimpered in fear and leaned away from him but the tent stayed firm. Shivering she waited for him to hit her but was shocked when all he did was bring her against his own shuddering body and hold her to him. Then he started to rock her back and forth while whispering softly in Dwarf the smell of his chain mail soothing her.

    The heat from his body broke the ice that gripped her. With a heart-rending cry she leaned against his chest her shaking fingers gripping his beard tightly.

The Dwarf whispered gently into her hair, " I am Braun. You are safe now. I will not let anyone hurt you like this again. Never again."

Confused, Savanna asked, " Why?"

She pulled back enough so she could look into his tear-streaked face. " Why would you protect me? You think I'm a mage sent to spy on you."

Braun smiled down at her, " No. I see the truth in your blood. We are connected through blood. Even now I feel what you feel. I am linked to you through the blood. Never will you be alone again."

" But Lord Oran?" Savanna shuddered as her mind shrank from the memory of what he had almost done to her and from the duel emotions that still raged within her that turned her blood to ice.

Braun looked behind him at the other two Dwarves. " They harm you they harm me. As I said I am linked to you."

Two throats groaned at his words. They were not happy with this revelation and Lord Oran looked like he wanted to hit something.

Braun stood up with her in his arms. His eyes glared at his friends. Then he carried her from the tent.

The moon was just sinking bellow the tree line. He carried her through the large crowd that had gathered outside. They parted to let them through with concern on their faces. He stopped long enough to ask, " Can someone bring a tub to my tent with hot water so that I can bathe her please?"

Several voices spoke up, " On the way." And, " Will she be alright?" and, " What happened?"

Braun walked silently through the throng of warriors. His eyes hard and filled with determination. The girl had hidden her face in his beard and was still shaking with reaction.

Savanna hid her face as soon as she saw all the warriors outside the tent. All those Dwarven faces looking at her had made her feel ashamed that they saw her in this state. Tremors still wracked her body from the trauma she had sustained inside the tent at Lord Oran's hands.

Many called out to them in Dwarf as they passed through the camp. Her head swam dizzily. She hoped her stomach would stay silent she didn't want to vomit on Braun. The taste of bile and blood was still on her tongue and she wanted something to get the taste out. In barely a whisper she croaked, " Tea, need some tea."

She felt Braun nod then he stopped and said something in Dwarf to someone walking next to him. There was a grunt and the sound of feet hurrying away.

Braun stopped twice more on his way to his tent. Both times he asked for stuff to be brought to his tent. He wanted clean clothing brought for the girl and food for both of them.

Savanna became aware that they were being followed by a large group of silent Dwarves. She could hear their heavy shuffling behind them. Then they were outside his tent and four Dwarves all dressed in black and silver armor stood outside the tent with two of them sporting dark scowling faces.

CHAPTER FOUR

They were met by four of the oldest Dwarves she had ever seen. Silver lined their long hair and beards. They nodded to Braun with grim faces as one of them held the flap open to let them into the tent. When he carried her inside she felt a jab of fear go through her when he placed her on her feet before them. Would these weathered old Dwarves hurt her as Lord Oran had?

They all stood around her looking her over like a prized horse in the light of the brazier and the lanterns two of them carried. They all scowled down at her then looked at Braun. They all wrinkled their noses.

Then one of them growled, " We need to talk but first you will bathe. I hate to say this child but you and Braun stink."

Savanna looked at the tub at the far side of the tent. Then heat flushed her face as she wondered if they meant to watch her as she bathed for there was no screen to hide behind. ***If they think I'm going to meekly bathe in front of them they will have a fight on their hands!*** Her hand went to her dagger only to find it gone. " Where's my dagger?"

The Dwarves grunted at the look she gave them. There was amusement in the eyes of the two shortest Dwarves as they exited the tent.

The last one to leave winked. " Just call us when you're done. Braun will use the communal bathes."

Braun nodded agreement at the old ones words. He pointed to the cot. " Those are for you to wear when you are done. I will be back as soon as I can." He took her hand in his and looked deeply into her eyes. "They will not harm you Savanna. Your dagger is in Oran's tent. I will get it when I am done bathing."

He grabbed up a set of garments for him-self before exiting the tent.

Alone Savanna looked questioning at the closed flap. He had told her she was safe with him but not why. Her mind still felt numb from her emotion storm.

Stripping she went to the tub. Naked she climbed into the hot bath water with a sigh of pleasure. ***This is the first hot bath I've had since before I left the village.***

She sank below the surface wetting her long hair. Sitting up she took up the soap and lathered her hair with it. She put the soap back onto the side table and once more sank below the surface to rinse out all the soap. Twice she did this until she was satisfied her hair was clean. Then she took the sponge and used the soap to lather it before scrubbing the rest of her clean. She didn't leave the tub until the water grew to cold for her to stay within it any longer. Getting out she saw that her fingers had puckered from the water.

A towel was folded neatly on the stool next to

the side table. She used it to dry her-self off. Wrapping the damp towel around her body she went to the cot. There on the covers was a clean black shirt and black leather breaches and was pleasantly surprised to find a comb for her hair. Smiling she put the garments on. The shirt was a bit big on her but the breaches molded to her every curve like a glove.

Taking the comb she went to the entrance and softly said, " I'm done."

Savanna quickly went and sat at the table to wait. She started to run the comb through her hair but it had been a long time since she had used one and the knots that had accumulated over the years proved troublesome. Gritting her teeth she started at the ends and slowly worked upwards.

She had only gotten a few inches into her hair when the flap opened and Braun entered with a large tray heaped with both food and drink. The same four Dwarves followed him inside.

Her heart raced in fear at seeing them. Five silver and black armored males made a very intimidating sight.

Braun placed the tray upon the table and seeing her struggling with the task of combing her hair chuckled and went to her aid. He gently took the comb from her and handed her dagger into her startled hand as he took over combing the mess her blond hair had become.

Savanna stiffened up at first as someone besides her-self handled her hair. Then when he didn't hurt her she relaxed. She found she enjoyed the feel of someone else combing her hair and relaxed further. Her hands clutched her dagger tightly in her lap.

Two of the Dwarves smiled kindly at her from across the table. One of them poured her a cup of tea and handed it to her. The other loaded a plate with meat and cheese and tore a piece off the loaf of bread and laid it on top before setting it in front of her. The other two sat and scowled at Braun as he continued to comb the knots from her hair.

Her hands shook as she sipped the tea. Wide eyed she watched them. The tea took the last of the foulness from her tongue and her stomach rejoiced by growling loudly inside the tent to her embarrassment. Which then caused Braun and the two smiling Dwarves to chuckle softly.

Blushing she hesitantly took a piece of cheese and slowly consumed it. Then she picked at the meat. Then back to the cheese and a bite of bread. She washed it down with tea. Before long her plate was empty and she was on her third cup of tea.

She blinked in surprise at the empty plate before her. Her hunger must have been great for her to eat every thing right down to the last crumb. She blushed in embarrassment.

While she had been eating they had been talking with Braun in Dwarf. What ever had been said seemed to satisfy the older ones.

" To get a better footing I think introductions are in order." The one on her left grinned. " I am Garn and this is Moag." He pointed to each as he named them. " Beldin and Garth. You already know our nephew Braun."

She bowed her head politely at the Dwarves. Her head spun dizzily. She blinked to clear her eyes but that only made her head spin even more. With a shaking hand she brought it to her head as she broke into a cold sweat. ***What is wrong with me?***

Braun steadied her as she started to sway. Then as suddenly as it hit it was gone. Her head cleared and her eyes refocused. She blinked at them from a pallid face.

" You okay?" Braun asked her with worry in his eyes. He had come to crouch in front of her. His eyes looked deeply into hers.

" Was a bit dizzy for a moment." She told him giving him a shaky smile. " Must still be tired."

Moag grunted and said, " The questions can wait until she regains her strength."

Garn patted her hand and nodded. " Sorry child. We had hoped to answer all your questions. Moag is right you need to rest and we oldsters can hold our curiosity far more then the young can."

Then he chuckled wickedly as he got up from the table. His eyes sparkled with amusement. " I will leave you with this answer before we depart."

Looking down at her he grinned from ear to ear then he said, " Welcome to the family Niece."

Niece? Savanna stared up at him in surprise. Her mouth dropped opened in a shocked " Oh."

He gently patted her cheek. Then still chuckling left the tent.

Moag snorted. " No tact that one."

He shook his head as he got up and came to her side. He took her hand and kissed her fingers lightly. " Braun can fill you in on all the details. You don't need us old Dwarves confusing you more than you already are."

With that he left them alone in the tent followed by the other two who still scowled only now she could see that their eyes twinkled in amusement.

Savanna looked at Braun. Her onyx eyes full of unspoken questions.

Braun stood up and held out his hand to her. Then smiled warmly when she took his hand with her cool one. " Come."

Savanna stood up and let him lead her to his cot her dagger gripped tight in her other hand. He gently sat her upon it and then he sat next to her. She waited for him to speak for she didn't trust her voice to stay steady if she started. Her heart was overwhelmed with mixed emotions.

" When I tasted your blood today. It told me who your mother was. She came from the mountains of Teirnan. She's a powerful Green Mage.." He looked sadly into her eyes. " You spoke truth when you told us she wanted to kill you and your twin at birth. What stayed her hand was an old seer that lived in the same village. He told her that if she raised her hand in violence to either of you she would be struck dead before her hand fell. So she let the two of you live. She never loved you or your twin."

Savanna found it hard to breath around the old grief that clutched her heart. She was unaware of the tears rolling unnoticed down her pale face.

Braun looked at her with sorrow filling his eyes. " I saw the death of your twin at the hands of a dark hooded figure. Saw his last moments and heard his last thoughts. He thought of you all alone wondering what happened to him."

Savanna chocked back a sob as her grief took hold of her. She had been the one who found his body. Closing her eyes she remembered the mutilated remains that had been her twin. " I found him. What was left of him after the animals got through with him."

He gently gripped her hands. Nodding he continued. " Yes, I know your blood showed me that as well. I also saw that you were being hunted and saw the words written on his chest. Who was hunting you can only be the same dark hooded one that followed your mother and killed your twin."

Fear grew inside her at his words. She looked at him with wide frightened eyes.

His heart lurched upon seeing and feeling that fright within her. "Your of the blood. My blood. Your safe within the family now."

Savanna looked at him in surprise. " How are we family?"

She had wanted to ask that question ever since Garn had named her niece.

Braun smiled into her eyes. " The blood showed me your father. It tried to hide the truth from me but I got angry and demanded to know." Braun closed his eyes but his face showed his anguish. " Your father is Gorn son of Broag."

Savanna shook. Her eyes widened at this revelation and her chest ached with suppressed emotion. All she could do was look up at him with tear filled eyes. *I know my father's name!*

" I'm your half brother. Braun son of Gorn" He told her quietly as his own tears rolled down his face. " I'm sorry I didn't stop Oran from hurting you. I was still held by your blood, still seeing all that had happened to you. By the time I realized what he was doing I got overwhelmed by your emotions and went berserk. That was when Gavan grabbed me and kept me from killing my best friend."

Savanna reached out trembling fingers and touched the wetness of his tears on his quivering face. His anguish made her heart break even more.

" Can you ever forgive me?" He whispered down at her. His dark eyes pleading.

" I have a brother?" She whispered in a chocked voice. With a cry she hugged him. *I have a brother! I'm not alone!*

Braun held her in his arms. Once more they shared tears as they found solace in one another. He kissed the top of her head breathing in the smell of soap. They stayed that way until he felt her hold slacken and light snores told him she was asleep. He chuckled softly as he gently laid her out on his cot. Covering her with blankets he sat on the edge watching her.

    Braun made up a mat across the entrance and with a sigh changed into his nightclothes. He faced her as he laid his head upon the cloak he had wrapped up for his pillow. *This is going to be an interesting night. I just hope I don't get trapped within her nightmares if she has any.*

CHAPTER FIVE

Oran watched as his friend carried the girl from his tent. He burned as if he stood right next to a forge. The urge to take the girl still raged within him. ***This cannot be happening! Not with her! Father is going to kill me!***

" Oran?" Gavan chocked out next to him. " Are you okay?"

Oran turned to his brother and snarled viciously. " No!" ***I would have raped her!***

Gavan saw something in his brother's face that made him rock back on his heals. The fire that burned in Oran's eyes spoke volumes. Every muscle tensed as if ready to spring into violence. The deep scratches the girl had given him still bled. " Those scratches need to be taken care of."

Oran growled dangerously at his words. His eyes narrowed. He tried to control the urge to smash his clenched fist into his brother's face.

" You need to leave." He told Gavan menacingly. " I will look after my wounds. Just go." Then shouted, " Go!"

Gavan left the tent quickly, leaving the ointment and bandages upon the table and quickly taking the girl's dagger with him shutting the tent flap behind him, but still Oran saw the crowd of Dwarves outside. Growling he looked at the cot in rage. His body still burned from the heat the girl had given off. With a snarl he took his anger and frustration out on the offending cot. ***Damn her!***

Oran ripped the covers off it and hurled them at the entrance. What was left of the ropes that the girl had burned off of her he left where they were. Then he went to the tub and taking the cloth started to mop up the girls vomit from the tent floor. Back and forth from the tub he went washing and rinsing until the floor was clean.

Picking up the covers he threw them outside and snarled at the closest Dwarf in russet armor, " Burn these and bring me fresh ones." Then closed the flap to shut out the crowd of scowling Dwarves outside his tent.

Oran paced the full length of the tent. Back and forth he went trying to cool his burning blood. His hand ached where the girl had bitten him. So to did his face. She had almost gotten his eyes with her nails.

The flap to his tent moved back and clean covers were thrust inside. Who ever had brought them stayed on the other side of the flap and as soon as the covers were out of their hands had closed the flap shut. The sound of heavy feet moving away told him they had left. He had seen the area around his tent was empty of Dwarves, they had all found other places to be.

The moon had also sunk low making the tent darken in match for his mood. He washed the blood from his hand and face. Then he smeared his wounds with the ointment Gavan had left on his table with clean bandaging. It stung as the ointment burned into each scratch and burned longer in the bite mark. Gasping in pain he then wrapped his right hand in the clean bandages.

Done he looked at the mess his tent had become. He then took the covers and placed them on the cot. Every time he touched it his blood burned with the memory of the girl bucking under him and his loins tightened even more until he was gasping in pain. ***Damn her!***

He reached into his breaches and found the source of his pain. ***Damn her! Got to stop this! Can't take any more! Hurts so much!***

Hand gripped and loosened then gripped again. His breathing deepened and his body shook with the need to find release. His pain increased but with it came pleasure hot and fluid. His rhythm quickened. He felt hot liquid flow over his hand but knew that he wasn't even close yet. Images of her beneath him flashed through his head. Pleasure increased and soon his hips were moving with the rhythm of his hand. He dug his nails into his flesh to call forth the seed as it rose deep within him and almost sobbed when it exploded forth in a shower of fluid, pleasure so intense he saw sparks dance before his eyes. His body jerked with every spasm. More fluid burst forth sending his orgasm even higher his body shuddering with pleasure.

Oran lay dazed upon the cot. His hand still clutched his now shrinking member. His night pants and hand were soaked with his seed. ***Damn her!***

Oran stumbled from the cot. He went to his chest and took out a fresh pair of breaches. He took the wet ones off and looked at his now empty member as if it was its fault in the first place. With a sigh he wiped his flesh down then put the clean breaches on.

The night was almost over dawn not far off. He sat at his table with a fresh bottle of spiced rum. With a growl he drank the rum straight from the bottle. *I almost raped her!* The alcohol hit him hard for he hadn't eaten since that morning and he had barely touched the plate of food still sitting in front of him. His head swam and so did his vision. *I almost raped her!* He looked down at his hands. *I will never touch her like that again!* His hands shook. *I won't force her never take her in force as long as I live! I will not rape her!*

His parents were going to kill him for this. He chuckled without humor. Now he knew why he found her familiar. She was his soul mate! A male of the blood could breed with any female of the blood unless his soul mate was found. Then he could only breed with her and none other. The girl his parents had chosen for him was dead to him now. His body wouldn't awaken to her no matter what she did. *Soul mate! Damn her! Damn me! Ah hell, Gavan's going to die laughing over this.*

He finished the bottle and then stumbled to the cot. Memory flitted in his mind and he swore he could still smell her hair. With that he passed out.

Gavan headed straight for Braun's tent with the girl's dagger in his hand. His mind roiling with the repercussions of what he had just witnessed. He needed to know if the girl was going to be all right. His heart ached for both his brother and for the girl the duel conflict warring inside him.

The reaction his brother had towards the girl spoke volumes. Never had he seen his brother lose control like that ever. **My god he almost raped her!** There was only one possible answer to that loss of control and his mind veered violently from that with a shudder.

If it is what I think it is, father is going to have a litter of kittens. Not to mention mother's hysterics. Savanna's reaction upon learning this, if it was so, was going to be chaotic to say the least especially on top of what she had just gone through. Damn this is going to be messy!

Braun was just exiting his tent when Gavan approached through the crowd of Dwarves. Their eyes met and with a mutual nod walked together in silence towards the communal baths the moon had sunk behind the trees and only the lantern in Braun's hand lit their way.

The communal bath was empty at that hour so they had privacy for the discussion that then took place as Braun hung the lantern and then stripped and entered one of the tubs.

" How is Savanna?" Gavan asked emotionlessly as he closely watched his friends face. The dark scowl

Braun gave him told him it wasn't good.

"Traumatized." Braun told him bluntly. Then spat. " What Oran did to her goes against every thing the Blood stands for! Gods Gavan he was going to rape her right before our eyes!"

Gavan nodded his agreement. " I fear it may be worse than that." He grimaced, " If my suspicions are correct we may have a volatile situation on our hands."

Braun looked at him with a snarl. " You don't think what happened to her wasn't volatile enough!" He glared dangerously up at his friend from the water. His fists clenched. " He was going to rape her!"

Gavan sighed. He wasn't looking forward to being a bearer of bad news, but his hunch gave him no choice. " I think Oran has soul bonded to the girl." Then waited for the explosion.

It came with Dwarven curses and much splashing as Braun stood angrily in the tub. Suds rolling down his body unnoticed in his rage. " Bloody Hell!" Water splashed as he slipped and fell back into the water sputtering in rage. " Hell he is!"

Gavan watched the myriad of emotions sweep over Braun's face. He waited for his friend to come to the realization of what that truly meant for Oran and Savanna.

" Ah hell!" Braun looked at Gavan with tears in his eyes. " She may also be blood bonded to him as well."

Gavan was shocked at that revelation. His eyes

widened. " Are you sure?"

Braun growled slapping the water in vexation. " Will know soon enough." Pain filled his eyes. " She took a lot of his blood when she bit him. I only hope she vomited all of it out."

" Does she have that gift to read the blood like you?" Gavan asked him softly.

Braun groaned and closed his eyes and nodded. " It runs in her bloodline from her great-grandmother. Her mother and grandmother didn't have it. I'm hoping it skipped her as well but won't know for sure."

Gavan sat on the bench next to the tub with a distressed groan. This situation was getting worse by the minute as they talked.

Braun groaned and sank bellow the water. He was linked to the girl and wasn't looking forward to the emotional storm that was surely going to take place between Savanna and Oran. He wouldn't be able to block the girl's emotions out. ***Hell if she and Oran join… I better be far away when that happens or have a willing female at hand to bed quickly.***

Gavan started to chuckle softly to himself as the implications of Oran's situation truly coming to light.

" I don't see anything funny about this situation." Braun snarled at him as he once more stood up in the tub. He glared at Gavan as he stepped out of the tub and toweled his skin dry.

Gavan chortled. " Don't you?"

Braun glowered as Gavan laughed even harder.

He had just fastened his breaches and was starting to pull his shirt over his head when it clicked into place.

" Oh." Braun sank to the bench next to Gavan surprise raising both brows into his hairline. " Oh, now I understand."

Both of them looked at each other with wickedly twinkling eyes. Then both of them burst into wild guffaws at the irony of the situation. Upon hearing their laughter those Dwarves outside raised questioning brows at their humor.

Both had tears of laughter running down their faces when they started to talk about Savanna.

" Did you see her burn those ropes off to scratch his face with her nails?" Braun chuckled wickedly at Gavan. He couldn't keep the pride from showing as he related his point of view. " She was like a wild animal even to taking a chunk out of his hand."

They both laughed even harder.

" Did you see the look on Oran's face when she got free and started to attack him?" Gavan snickered evilly. " That was truly priceless!"

" Had warned him she was feisty." Braun snickered. " Now we get to see just how feisty she is when we get back to the Mountain Holt."

Gavan looked at him in surprise. " Get back?"

Braun snickered. " My uncles want her safe at the Holt. They think a female of the family belongs with other females of the family. Garn was adamant about sending her to my mother for training in her healing gift."

Gavan added up the time and his eyes widened more in amusement. " Oran's would be bride will be arriving at the Holt soon if she's not already there."

Once again they howled with laughter at the irony. Together they left the communal bath and headed back to Braun's tent.

" Well I have to get back to the tent of healing." Gavan sighed as they stopped outside the tent he handed over the girl's dagger. " Give my regards to Savanna. Send her over in the morning for training in her gift. She needs it."

CHAPTER SIX

Savanna found her-self looking out of another's eyes. She saw Gavan and Braun. They were young just starting to grow their beards. All of them were full of mischievous troublemaking. They were sneaking into a tunnel that had been deemed off limits to younglings.

" Shhhh!" The one she rode said as the other two started to giggle at their own temerity. " Do you want Moag to hear us?"

Braun snorted. " My uncle would be the first to turn a blind eye on our adventure."

Gavan laughed. " Besides every one is at the great hall for the feast."

The young Dwarves went on in silence. They would stop every once in awhile to listen for voices either ahead or behind them for voices carried differently in the tunnels. Going left into another tunnel then right then left again. Soon they were getting closer to their destination for they came here often to swim. The waters were warm from the volcanic heat far bellow that kept the waters warm.

They entered the cavern that held the hot spring. The metallic smell of the water filled the air around them. They put their lanterns on the shelf next to the pool. All three lanterns lit the room enough for them to see all the walls clearly.

Savanna marveled at the beauty. Jeweled tones glowed with the lantern light. Some of the light reflected and split into tiny shards of rainbow hues. She knew she dreamed but this dream wasn't hers.

The one she rode began to strip and so two did Gavan and Braun. Seeing her brother naked felt wrong and she tried to avert her eyes but the one she rode held her in place as if she wasn't even there looking out of his eyes.

Then all of them went to the water. The one she rode looked into the water and she knew now whose eyes she looked out of. In shock she saw a much younger Lord Oran looked back at her from the rippling waters surface. The beginnings of a beard were starting to cover his face.

They swam for some time. Enjoying the thrill of swimming in an area deemed off limits. They chased each other on top of the water and below its shinning surface.

Suddenly Savanna felt fear. Something was wrong but the young Dwarves didn't notice. She wanted to warn them but couldn't. Her mind screamed for the one she rode to take notice but he was oblivious to her.

Then it struck!

Dark swirling limbs came out of the water and wrapped around Gavan. His face went white in shock and terror as the thing pulled him under the water.

Braun shouted, " Gavan!"

He dove under and so to did Oran. Together they saw the monster that had made the pool his home. Now they knew why the pool had been deemed off limits.

They went at the monster together.

All of them swam with their knives on. Now those knives were used to slash at the arms that held Gavan. Only going to the surface for that precious breath of air then diving back to do battle.

The monster thrashed as they cut deep with each slash of their knives. Then the thing let Gavan go and with a swoosh of black fluid it vanished into the depths of the pool.

Together they pulled Gavan to the edge of the pool. They were worried for he didn't move. Together they dragged him out of the water and mindful of the monster carried him to the farthest part of the cavern.

Oran cried hoarsely as he thumped his brother's chest.

Savanna felt his grief and fear as well as his guilt for it had been his idea to go swimming here even though their father had warned them to stay away. *I should have listened! Come back Gavan! Don't leave me!*

Braun gathered their clothing and already dressed told Oran to dress while he thumped Gavan to get him to breath out the water he had brought into his lungs.

Oran had just finished dressing when Gavan came up chocking and vomiting water. Then they all shook at how close they had come to getting killed. Both Oran and Braun helped Gavan to dress. Then they swore never to return to this cavern until the elders deemed it safe to do so.

Savanna heard Oran silently swear *I will never bring my brother into danger ever again!* Her heart went out to the young Oran.

Her dream shifted and she found her-self standing in a great cavern filled with Dwarven warriors dressed for battle in array of colors, black and silver, dark brown, russet, white, and blue. Once more she looked out of Oran's eyes but this time he was an adult. She felt his fear though he didn't show it and she felt his excitement as well.

Strength filled his muscles and the weight of the axe at his side was comforting. His father had given it to him last evening as his birthing gift.

Savanna watched as a massive Dwarf in russet armor stood upon a platform of onyx. His eyes roved the massed Dwarves before him then came to rest upon Oran. She felt Oran stand taller and his mind whispered in pride, *Father!*

Once again her dream shifted. Oran's anger filled her as he stood before his parents. His body trembled with his emotions. *Never!*

" She will bring harmony to our two families." His mother told him gently her dark eyes looking at him through the veils that covered her face.

His father glared at him. He was not happy with his son's response to the news. " This betrothal will happen." He told his son. " Her father Dwarf King Thorin of Halvorn Mountain has agreed to the terms.

This will merge the two bloodlines and will bring piece to both our mountains. You will marry her."

" No!" Oran almost shouted as he denied both his parents. " I will not marry her!"

His father roared in rage. " You will marry her in one year! Until that time I am sending you to learn humility at Argon Pass as Commander of the Thirteenth Company!"

The dream shifted again and this time Savanna found her-self locked in battle with a very large man. Sword clanged against axe as they met. Sparks flew from the meeting of metal on metal.

Oran strained against the taller and heavier foe. He growled as he shifted his weight and went under the swing of his opponent and his axe found the flesh of the man's belly. Blood lust sang through his veins.

The man gasped in shock as his innards came tumbling out with a gush of blood. He staggered back and stared stupidly at Oran as he dropped his sword and tried to stuff his entrails back into the gapping wound.

Oran swiftly brought his axe around and clove the man's head from his body. He watched dispassionately as the body fell twitching onto the ground. Then he turned to see Braun behead his opponent just as pain exploded in his shoulder. He looked in amazement at the arrow sticking from his flesh.

Once more the dream shifted. By this time Savanna knew this to be Oran's memories. She felt dread at what would be revealed to her this time.

She saw her-self on the cot. Straining to get free wildly thrashing and screaming as Lord Oran held her down. Saw her-self bite his hand and felt his pain and arousal then felt his molten heat fill him and his member as the ropes binding her wrists burst into flames and her nails raked his face.

She felt his turmoil of mixed emotions. This time she heard his thoughts as well as he gripped her wrists and wrapped his hand into her hair.

Lord she feels good. Shouldn't feel this with her. No! This can't be happening! His face went ugly as his body responded to her thrashing and even the sting of her nails sent a shiver of desire through his already boiling blood. Denial slammed into her. **Is this why she feels familiar? No! She can't be!**

Savanna gasped as she felt his arousal fill her. Deep inside her own body responded with its own arousal in answer. Now she too cried out in denial at the wanting that rose mindlessly through her. Felt his body start to harden as she tried to buck him off and felt his need slam into her making her gasp in shock. Felt his pleasure rise inside her then explode into a pleasure so intense she shook from it. Every nerve ending in her body sang with pleasure and burned with need.

Savanna fought free of the dream/memory. Truth slammed into her. She shook with it. The blood she had swallowed when she had bitten Lord Oran had linked him to her as her blood had linked Braun to her.

Even now she could feel him. Feel his emotions of intense pleasure mixed with pain filling her. She looked at the tent wall as she shook in arousal every nerve in her body humming. Even now her body ached for his touch. ***No! I cannot be wanting him! This can't be happening!*** But the truth burned within her. ***I took his blood. Gods forgive me. I feel him!*** She closed her eyes in revelation for his blood showed her the truth. ***Soul mate!*** His pleasure intensified within her then her head exploded as his orgasm slammed into her making her almost swoon. Her nether regions throbbed in response as her belly tightened painfully in reaction. ***Oh my!***

Shaken and unable to sleep Savanna quietly left the cot. The brazier glowing softly on the floor showed Braun on a mat across the entrance looking at her with thoughtful eyes.

With a grimace she said, " I think I have a problem."

Going to the table she took a seat as Braun grunted as he got up to join her. She watched as Braun lit the lantern on the table illuminating the tent. He was in a long nightshirt and pants. His long ebony hair framed his face like a halo and his black beard was mussed up.

Savanna looked nervously down at her hands. ***How do I begin?***

Taking a deep breath she whispered, " I think I'm linked to Lord Oran."

She trembled as she waited for his response to that worded bomb. When he only gently took her hands into his did she look up at him with pain and unshed tears. " It must have happened when I bit his hand and gotten his blood in my mouth."

" I was fearing this when I saw you bite him." Braun told her gently. " That is why I took you here to my tent." He shook his head sadly as he gazed into her eyes. " I didn't know what you would see through his blood and I was hoping that you had vomited it all out." *I also hoped to be miles away so I wouldn't feel your arousal! The Gods must be laughing at me.*

Savanna closed her eyes as more visions swept through her. She saw his birth, the faces of his mother and sisters, his grandfather and more. Her head swam with his memories and with his emotions.

" Easy now." Braun squeezed her fingers giving her something to home in on. " You didn't get this gift from our father. Your mother gave you this gift even though it skipped her. This gift is strong in your mother's line. Your great-grandmother had it." *I had hoped it would have skipped you as well wishful thinking on my part.*

Savanna looked at him in almost a double vision the two visions over lapping each other. " How long?"

Braun shrugged his shoulders. " Don't know. It depends on how strong the gift is and the amount of blood taken. Can be a few hours or even a few days at the most."

Savanna groaned at his words. She wasn't looking forward to suffering through his memories any longer than she had to. Hopefully they would be gone in a few hours not days.

" I will help you through this. I can't see what you see but I can feel what your feeling." He told her with a wry smile. *What I'm feeling right now is going to the village to fall into the arms of the first Doxy that smiles!*

Savanna grimaced. " That doesn't seem like much fun for either of us." Then remembering what she had just experienced she blushed deeply in mortification. She was still aroused. *Defiantly not fun! Got to find out if there's a way to block this or Braun's going to go nuts every time this happens*.

Braun chuckled as his eyes glimmered with humor. " Nope."

" Are you still seeing visions from my blood?" She asked. *I hope not!* Then almost panicked. *How much has he seen?*

" No. Those stopped a little while ago but I will feel your emotions all the time. That won't go away ever." He told her as he patted her hands.

" So I will feel Lord Oran's emotions all the time as well." Savanna grimaced. " As if my life isn't difficult enough as it is." She grumbled chagrined.

Braun laughed at her sally. Her spunk was coming back. " There are advantages to this you know." He chuckled wickedly. " You will always know where he is so you can avoid him if that is your wish but in this camp that can be very difficult to do."

Then he chuckled, " You will also be able to take advantage of those emotions."

" Especially if he gets injured again." Savanna sighed dramatically then her eyes widened. " Would I feel his pain if he's injured?"

Braun shrugged his shoulders. " Don't know. This is the first time I ever read some ones blood. If you want I can punch him tomorrow and see if you feel it?"

Savanna's eyes blazed into his. " Don't you dare! He will want to know why you hit him and I don't want him knowing that I am linked to him!"

Braun roared in laughter.

Savanna blushed. She would die of embarrassment if Lord Oran knew she could feel his emotions. Thinking of his reaction to that knowledge gave her the shivers. No she didn't want him to know about her connection to him. ***It would be safer if he never found out.***

Still chuckling Braun asked. " How are you feeling now?"

Savanna was surprised to realize that the double vision had gone and she was once more wanting to go back to sleep. " Better. The visions are gone but I still feel him."

Braun nodded. " That is good. You think you can go back to sleep now."

Savanna yawned in answer to his question. This made him chuckle and shoo her back to the cot to sleep.

"We will talk more in the morning. Our uncles will be joining us for breakfast. By now the entire Company knows you're of the blood. There is going to be a lot of curious Dwarves hanging around to catch a glimpse of you come morning." He told her with a chuckle as he extinguished the light and climbed back into his mat by the entrance. "Good night Savanna."

"Good night Braun." She answered softly. Her heart clenched at the thought of all those curious Dwarven faces looking at her when morning arrived. *Would they react as Lord Oran had or would they be more like Braun?*

"Stop worrying Savanna." Braun growled at her from the darkness. "They will not hurt you. Now get some sleep."

With a sigh Savanna closed her tired eyes and fell into a dreamless sleep.

CHAPTER SEVEN

Savanna held her anger in check as Garth told Braun that she would be going to the Mountain Holt sometime in the next few days. Her eyes glared at her clenched hands as she sat quietly fuming at the breakfast table. They had no idea she could now understand and speak Dwarf.

Some how the blood she had taken from Lord Oran had opened her to the language. So when Garth spoke to Braun in Dwarf about sending her to the Holt she had understood them and decided to let them talk over her as if she didn't understand what they said.

She saw the advantage to this deception instantly. The Dwarves would never speak openly around her if they knew she understood. So she kept her new found secret and learned from the unchecked talk around her. She had to bite her tongue frequently to keep herself from speaking out with indignation at their plans for her.

" Lord Oran should be getting a summons home any day now." Moag chortled as he wiped the last of his eggs from his plate. " His betrothed should have arrived and the wedding planning in full swing by now. We will send her with him when the time comes."

" Do you think that wise?" and " Are you crazy?" and from Braun, " Not alone!" rang out around the table startling the Dwarf.

Moag snorted in indignation as his dark eyes

flashed at those who had spoken out. " Of course not alone! You think I'm going to trust him alone with her after what he did to her? Braun will be going with them."

Savanna felt her heart race at his words and both anger and frustration made her fingers curl. She wanted to pull the girls hair out and scratch her face off and at the same time her heart clenched and heat swirled through her belly making it quiver with the thought of being alone with Lord Oran.

Confused by her feelings she had no right to feel she would have left the table if Braun hadn't patted her hand gently and look into her face with sympathy.

" I will teach you our language." He told her with kindness and understanding in his dark eyes. " It must be frustrating to have us talk over you like this."

" The sooner the better." Garth agreed his eyes aglow with warmth.

" Here! Here!" Rang out around the table as every one smiled at her. None of them even guessed at her true feelings except Braun who was smirking at her. If they had they wouldn't be smiling at her they would be angry instead and demanding answers that she herself didn't know.

Her changing feelings for Lord Oran mystified her. Could his blood have changed her that much? She didn't want to probe to deeply into her feelings for fear of what she might find. No way was she ready to delve that deeply into her soul and she feared the truth that would be revealed if she did. Her heart whispered ***he's mine!*** Her head ***No!***

" You will like my mother." Braun told her with sparkling eyes as he broke her from her confusion. " She will help with your training."

Savanna was startled. " Training?"

Braun grinned widely at her. " Yes. Training. She will teach you all about our way of life and help you to control your gifts."

Savanna wondered what else his mother would train her in and blushed as her mind envisioned possible scenarios some of which were in dealing with males.

" Gavan wishes for you to come to the tent of healing for your training with your healing gift." Braun told her as he rose from the table. " He figures you can use the practice before leaving."

Savanna pretended confusion at his words. " Leaving? Where am I going?"

Braun sighed and said. " Forgive me I forgot that part of the conversation was in Dwarf. My uncles are sending you to the Mountain Holt in a few days to place you into the knowing hands of my mother."

" Why?" Savanna now let her anger show. " I am needed here. My gift of healing will be needed in the up coming battles. Now is not the time to send me away!"

The others looked at her sternly.

" I am your elder child." Garth told her sternly. His eyes brooked no argument as he glared at her from the table. " You will go to the Holt!"

She was about to snap back when Braun squeezed her arm in warning. Looking into his face he shook his head. Knowing she was out numbered she gave in but her eyes threw sparks at the silver and black armored males before her as she hissed. " As you wish."

Savanna stormed from the tent. She was unaware of the sight she had made upon leaving. Dark eyes blazed with anger and her small frame ramrod straight and defiance in her very stance in black flowing shirt and breaches that molded to her legs for she gave up on her dresses. One hand on the hilt of her dagger the other on her hip for she had taken to wearing it in full sight upon her thigh.

Garns eyes glimmered with amusement as he watched the girl storm from the tent. " There's fire in that one."

The others chuckled as appreciation glowed in all their eyes.

" It will take a very strong male to harness all that fire." Moag agreed chuckling. " Did you see what she had done to Oran's face and hand?"

Braun almost chocked on his tea.

They all laughed for they had seen what she had done to him. Pride in the girl swept through them all especially seeing she was of their blood.

Braun hadn't told them she had done it to keep Oran from raping her. He didn't want them challenging his friend and their superior to combat for the girl's honor until he was sure of the bonding the two may share.

" I think the others will take note that she's not as week as she looks." Beldin chuckled as he took another bite of bread. His eyes glistened with amusement. " There's going to be fights before this year is done."

" Mmmf!" Garth snorted. Eyes twinkling with suppressed mirth. " There's going to be many fathers coming to bid for her for their worthy sons."

Moag chuckled, " Not to mention their wives going to our wives hoping for an advantage that way. Once they learn she is gifted there's going to be a shift in power among the females."

Braun listened to their rambling over the girl. He saw another path that could very well cause war among the blood. They needed to see all the paths that lay before the girl's feet even the bad. " They may even call her cursed."

Silence met his words. Their eyes looked at him in query almost dangerous.

" Why would you say that?" Moag growled his hand fell to the hilt of his sword.

" She is not only of the blood but of the blood of Teirnan as well." Braun told them with hard eyes. " There will be those who won't see passed that blood. Some may even condemn her for it and cause trouble for the girl. We need to be vigilant about her safety for there is still one out there that hunts her even now."

They all grunted and nodded at his words for they saw the truth within them. Five pares of eyes gleamed fiercely as hands lay upon their weapons. They had all accepted her as one of their own and would defend her to their last breath.

Savanna reached the tent of healing in time to see Lord Oran leaving it. Her heart nearly stopped when their eyes met. She had almost walked right into him. They were so close she could smell his heavy musk it made her head swim uncomfortably and her belly to tighten with desire hot and molten within her.

Hot desire mixed with self-anger and guilt slammed into her as Oran's emotions filled her. Shocked by the storm coming from him she touched his face with her fingers and he stood calmly at her touch though from his emotions he was anything but calm.

Her heart once more growled **Mine!** She ignored it.

She had done this to him. Her own guilt made her eyes bright with unshed tears. She ran her fingers lightly over the scratches. Looking into his eyes she wondered why he let her touch him and saw that his eyes burned with the emotions she was sensing from him.

" Forgive me." She whispered then healed the injuries she had caused. The scratches vanished and so to did the injury upon his hand where she had bitten him.

Oran once again felt the power flow through him from her fingers. The sight of her all in black and with breaches that clung to her every curve had made his loins tighten uncomfortably and arousal had blazed through his blood. ***I wonder what she would look like in veils?***

Savanna watched as his eyes burned even brighter into hers. Her belly fluttered. Then her eyes dropped to his lips and her breath caught. She was transfixed as she watched him lick his lips and finding her own dry licked hers in reaction. ***Oh I think I'm in trouble here!***

" You play with fire girl." Oran warned her his voice almost savage to her ears. " You'll get burned."

"Yes." She said huskily as her hands found his beard and couldn't stop her-self from wrapping her fingers into its long silky black strands completely lost in the emotions swirling through her. With a strangled cry of pure need she pulled him to her. ***MINE!***

Oran groaned at the arousal that shown from her eyes. Her fingers gripping his beard had shocked him literally. The jolt of electricity that went through him took away his breath. He couldn't stop her from pulling him down.

Savanna groaned deep in her throat as she felt his lips on hers. A jolt of pure arousal so powerful zapped through her. With a gasp her mouth opened. She wanted more. ***MINE!***

Oran felt her mouth open with a gasp. He took

advantage and deepened the kiss. He found she tasted of honey and almonds. His arousal rose to a raging fire with in him but he kept his hands clenched at his sides.

How long they stood there kissing they didn't know for it was the chuckles around them that brought them both back to reality.

Shocked they pulled apart both trembling in reaction. Both of them were breathing hard and flushed as they looked around them.

Gavan stood looking at them from the entrance his brows raised into his hairline with surprise written all over his shocked face. Along with half a dozen grinning Dwarves staring at them many of which were chuckling and wagging brows at one another and catcalls hooted around them with raucous laughter.

Savanna blushed. She wanted to hide but there was nowhere to hide from this. It was she after all who had her hands wrapped tightly into Oran's beard. Shyly she looked up into his eyes and almost lost her breath. He gazed down at her with arousal burning in the depths of his dark eyes and a smile twitching at the corners of his lips. Oran was trying not to grin at her.

Oran didn't move. All he did was look hungrily down at the girl who owned his soul. Seeing the blush deepen in her face made his mouth twitch with the urge to smile but he didn't want to frighten her with his overwhelming emotions. She would have to make all the moves for he would never lay a hand upon her as he had before. If she wanted a kiss then she would have to initiate the kiss, if she wanted more than a kiss well there to she would have to force the issue. He would never try to force her ever again. All the moves would have to come from her but he would never deny her.

All this and more did Savanna read from him as she stared in wonder up into his eyes. She shook with the realization that this Dwarf was hers. Only problem was he was promised to another.

Her heart snarled *MINE!*

CHAPTER EIGHT

Oran stood guard at the entrance as he watched the girl go from warrior to warrior healing them with her gift. Her shirt flowed over large upon her small frame but the breaches molded to her legs making his loins tighten even more. The dagger now strapped to her thigh for all to see gave an almost warrior like appearance that made his lips twitch with humor.

He smiled at the surprised looks each one gave her as she healed them. The whispers of " Carra" (Healer) came from stunned lips.

Gavan walked with her. His eyes avidly watching every thing she did with interest. He to noted the whispers and smiled knowingly. This was the only way he knew to help solidify the girls standing with the Dwarves. For like Braun he to worried about her acceptance among the Dwarves within the Holt.

Oran had told him that he had received a letter from their father calling him back to the Holt. That the wedding was at hand and his presents was needed for the festivities. His blushing bride wanted her soon to be husband in attendance. The dark grimace Oran had given that news almost made Gavan laugh.

Now his heart went out to both Oran and Savanna when he had seen the heated kiss that obviously Savanna had initiated. He had seen the pain that shadowed her eyes with every glance she sent Oran's way. Telling him that she knew of the betrothal and had no idea what to do with her feelings for Oran which shown plainly for all to see.

    Oran knew the news of their kiss would spread through the camp like a grass fire. There would be many questions they would have to answer before the day was through especially from the girl's uncles. He would never let her face them alone. With his wounds healed he would be able to hold his own against the best of them if they should challenge him over this but he wasn't the one who initiated the kiss and over six Dwarves had witnessed it. Three of which were blood related to the girl.

    Savanna was oblivious to the consequences of the kiss they had shared. Her eyes and mind were filled with the healing of the wounded now that her gift was known. Power flowed unchecked from her fingers as she healed all she touched. She smiled down at the startled warriors as she healed them. There eyes widened and with trembling fingers had touched her face and whispered, " Carra."

    She smiled shyly down at them. Unaware that tears rolled down her cheeks and her emotions shone from her eyes full force. Each warrior breathed in awe at what they saw as she healed them as she passed, her tears landing upon a face, a hand, a chest. Behind her rose a soft chant of awe filled reverence of the name " Carra."

    Her uncles strode into the tent. They stopped in surprise at the scene before them. In stunned silence they watched as she went from warrior to warrior.

She shone brightly with a white light. Her sweet face smiling with a peaceful radiance as she gently touched each one healing the wounded right before their eyes and their ears filling with the chant. " Carra." That soon rose to a crescendo that filled the tent.

She stopped at the last warrior a human with a look of painful bemusement on his weathered face. He labored to breath for his was a lung shot the arrow still in his flesh. Into his bewildered face she smiled and said. " Fear not for even this cannot stay my hand."

With one hand she gripped the arrow and with the other she touched the base of the wound. Fire blazed over her skin and down the arrow it went into the wound it-self. Her head shot back in a silent scream as she pulled the arrow lose. The flames swirled over her body sweeping her hair in its silent wind. It blazed from her eyes making all who watched cry out!

Then it flowed into the warrior under her hand. His scream filled the tent and then the light was gone and with a soft moan the girl fainted into Gavan's trembling arms as he wept hoarsely.

The human shook as he saw the girl collapse in a dead faint. His wound was gone not a mark to show that it had ever been. The memory of the fire that had burned through him left him shaken to the core. With trembling fingers he touched her tear streaked face with wonder.

Oran swiftly strode to his brother and with a

grim look on his face took Savanna from his trembling arms. He then turned to face her shaken uncles that still blocked the entrance. His eyes shown with a predatory light as he walked purposely towards them. From his mouth came forth his bound oath. " I give my heart and soul to this female of thy Blood. For her only shall my seed flow. I bind my-self to this female even after death for only for her my seed will flow. I Oran son of Morgan Dwarf Lord of Magog do claim my soul mate before her kith and kin."

    Gravely the four elders of her bloodline bowed to him showing his right to claim her and moved aside to let him pass with his mate in his arms their eyes thoughtful as he strode from the tent.

    Gavan watched silently as his brother left with his soul mate in his arms. He shook his head then chuckled softly as he thought of their father and his reaction to this. The finding and claiming of a soul mate was higher than a betrothal. His father was definitely going to have a litter of kittens when he learned of this turn of events. Not to mention the bride waiting for his return to claim her as wife. The ripples this was going to cause when they returned to the Holt was definitely going to set fire to some egos.

    Oran once more placed her upon his cot. He then took the remains of the rope from the bed. He didn't want his mate to see them and be reminded of her first stay there.

    For the first time in his life he felt whole and

with a gentle hand he pushed her hair back off her sleeping face. For sleep she did with light snores rising from her. Pulling the covers over her he kissed her brow before going to the entrance.

He waved one of his aids over. A Dwarf dressed in the same russet leathers and armor as him. " Bring food and drink for me and my mate."

The Dwarf smiled at him. " Right away Lord Oran." Then with a jingling of chain mail trotted away.

Oran re-entered his tent and went to sit at his table. He picked up his fathers letter and reread it. The betrothal was now null and void with him claiming his soul mate. There was no need for him to go back to the Holt.

Taking fresh paper and refilling his inkbottle he then put quill to the paper and wrote his news to his father. He used the archaic form of address as was required by one who had found his soul mate. His words getting lengthy as it was required. Then he took a small penknife and let three drops of his blood fall to the paper as he spoke the ancient words of oath again and the blood glowed as it hit the paper burning symbols that only one of the Holy ones could read. That alone bound his oath in the eyes of the Gods none could break the oath now. Not even the burning of the paper could erase the oath he had spoken and written.

Oran looked once more upon the sleeping girl. One more oath to take the one she alone must hear and whether she liked it or not he was hers. Even if she denied him his soul and his seed would belong to her for that was the way of Dwarf males.

So he waited for her to wake.

The food arrived and he placed it upon the table.

Hunger filled him but he did not eat for this to was required until she woke and heard his oath then food would be ceremonially shared.

So he waited for her to wake.

The tent grew dark and he lit the lantern. Its light filling the tent with its glow.

And still he waited his eyes never leaving the sleeping girls face.

Then she stirred and slowly opened her eyes. He saw the recognition of her surroundings and her eyes fell on him they were wide and frightened. The urge to go to her was strong but his will was stronger than his need. He stayed in the chair and looked solemnly into her startled face as she sat up and moved to sit on the edge of the cot.

Savanna looked at him with mixed emotions rising inside her. ***Why is it that every time I faint I end up in his bed?***

" I will not go to you unless you wish it." Oran told her gently. " I need to say things to you but they need to be said near you, may I come to sit before you so that what is needed to be said can be said?" he asked her solemnly from his chair.

Savanna's eyes widened in surprise then

narrowed as suspicion rose within her. Still fearful but her curiosity grew with each word he told her. She sensed that he would sit there all night until she gave him permission to go to her.

" Please come sit near me so that you can speak what needs to be spoken." She told him gravely. It was beginning to feel ceremonial and this made her heart beat strangely within her.

Oran slowly made his way over to her then to her surprise he kneeled on the floor before her. Then as her eyes widened in shock he took his shirt off and placed it on the floor. Her mouth went dry as she saw his massive chest bare before her. Fear filled her when he took out a wicked looking knife.

Oran watched her eyes widen and narrow then widen again with each thing he did. He could see the fear and curiosity warring in her face and eyes. Which one would win he didn't know or care. He needed to say his oath to her and his blood must run to seal the oath into his flesh for all to see.

Savanna gasped when he took up the knife and cried out as she felt his pain when he sliced the flesh over his heart. His blood flowed freely right before her eyes. With a sob she reached to heal it but his eyes and voice held her transfixed.

" With the flow of my blood I bind my-self to you." Oran spoke gravely at her astonished ears in Dwarf. " I Oran son of Morgan Dwarf Lord of Magog give unto you my soul and my seed. For you alone do both belong even after death."

Blue fire blazed from the wound he had made. Even though it pained him greatly she saw him accept the pain as price for the words he had spoken. Her heart lurched as she felt that power flow through her as well. Then watched as the wound and the blood flowed into silvery Dwarf runes that formed a circle over his heart. She shook as she realized that he had bound him-self to her literally. With a sob she stared at him in shock.

Oran sat looking at her from the floor. He didn't touch her.

Savanna reached out and touched the runes that glowed newly upon his flesh. Her fingers trembled as she felt only hot skin beneath them. She looked into his solemn eyes and said the only thing that came to her mind. " Why?"

Oran answered her simple question as best as he could. " You are my soul mate."

Truth rang from his words making Savanna shake in reaction. ***Soul mate!*** He had bound him-self to her in blood just as she had bound him to her-self with his blood. There was only one thing she honorably could do.

Not knowing if the words would work for her she looked at him and said with tears shinning in her eyes. " I Savanna Daughter of Rainnon mage of Teirnan and Daughter of Gorn do accept thy soul and thy seed as belonging only to me. With the blood I took from thee I bind my soul and heart and all that I be to thee Oran son of Morgan Dwarf Lord of

Magog."

Power filled her and burned the flesh over her body. She gasped as the pain of invisible quills pierced her flesh from head to toe. She was dimly aware of Oran crying out to her but he didn't touch her for he sat in numbed shock.

CHAPTER NINE

Savanna gritted her teeth but refused to voice how much pain she was in. If he could suffer in silence then so to could she. How long the quills pierced her she didn't know for it felt like an eternity had passed but still she suffered in silence only her short gasping breaths was the only sound that filled the tent. Then it was over and her flesh burned from the memory of the pain.

Savanna found Oran weeping before her. His breathing ragged in her ears. He trembled uncontrollably with eyes wide in disbelief.

" What have you done?" He chocked at her. Confusion and anger blasted from him slamming forcefully into her unchecked making her blood freeze.

Savanna gasped. " You bound your-self to me was it not honorable for me to do it also?" then shivered chilled as she looked at the Dwarf runes blazing over every inch of exposed flesh. " Though I must admit mine are more dramatic then yours. Are they also upon my face?"

Oran closed his eyes and groaned. " Yes."

Savanna trembled as she thought how they must look upon her and tears glistened in her eyes. " Do I look hideous?"

She began to sob brokenly as she shivered with cold.

" Don't." Oran looked at her as his eyes

lingered on her face and smiled at her through his tears. " You are lovely. The runes enhance your beauty."

Shyly Savanna choked back her sobs. " But you wont touch me."

Oran groaned. " I swore never to touch you unless you tell me to."

Savanna's eyes widened as understanding dawned within her making molten heat replace the chill that had filled her. " Please touch me Oran."

Oran trembled at hearing her words. " I fear I won't be able to control my-self if I touch your fairness."

" Oran." She almost shouted at him her eyes flashing with temper heating her blood even more. " Damn you touch me!"

Oran groaned and reached out tentative fingers to trace a set of runes that swirled up her cheek and across her forehead to vanish into her hairline. His blood burned and he was about to draw his hand away when she grasped it and brought his hand to her wildly beating heart.

Savanna felt his need rising within him and felt her own need awakening in answer. Her blood burned wanting him to touch her. With her other hand she grasped his beard and brought his face up to meet hers as she leaned over to gently brush her trembling lips to his.

His mouth opened in shock at her kiss and he moaned her name as he deepened it. He needed to taste her honey and almonds. His tongue forced her mouth to open further and his tongue delved deeply into her mouth exploring and tangling with hers.

Savanna whimpered as he explored her mouth with his tongue. Jolts of pleasure swept through her at each thrust and flick as their tongues did a mystical dance within.

Her heartbeat quickened beneath his hand and her whimpers of pleasure made him groan as he shifted his body to ease the pain in his now throbbing member. ***Mustn't lose control! Gods she tastes good!***

Savanna wanted more. She wanted to touch his trembling flesh with her fingers. Releasing his hand over her heart she touched his chest and was surprised by the heat that burned in him. She ran her hand through the curling hair on his chest with gentle fingers and felt him stiffen at her touch. She stopped thinking she had hurt him. Then he leaned into her touch with a groan that filled her mouth and sent her mind spinning with arousal so powerful her body shook with it. She could feel his pain as his member swelled to its fullness. With a moan she trailed her hand slowly down his chest, making her way down his hard belly and even lower seeking his pain.

Suddenly Oran pulled back with a moaning cry. His arousal slammed into her full force and she could feel him struggling to control the heat that was boiling his blood. He was fighting his emotions his chest heaved as he fought for control.

Fire burned in the dark depths of his eyes, as he

gazed into her face. His eyes seeking something from her. " Savanna. My fire burns within me. If we don't stop now I will lose control." Then growled as if in pain. " I will not force you!"

Savanna burned as his words finally found purchase within her aroused fogged mind.

" Oran." She suddenly didn't want him to stop. His pain was now her pain. Her body ached violently in the very depths of her. " Oran please?"

" Savanna!" Oran growled savagely in answer to her plea. " You know not what you ask. There will be pain. I don't want to hurt you."

He gently took her face in his hands and kissed every part until he once more claimed her mouth. Then he pulled back and whispered. " Command me Savanna." He looked into her smoldering eyes. " Do you want me to stop?" emotions were conflicting within him. ***Say yes! Say no! Gods help me I'm lost!***

Gasping for breath around the furnace that had become her blood. Savanna cried out to him. ***I don't want this to end!***

" Help me Oran." She sobbed. She took his hand and placed it over her belly that ached deep within her. " It hurts Oran please help me."

Oran groaned and buried his face into her shoulder at the base of her throat as he fought for control over his arousal.

He could feel her pulse beating wildly against his lips. She shivered and with a cry she pressed her neck into his lips gasping and shaking uncontrollably.

That undid him! Control gone he pulled the shirt off of her. With a savage growl he trailed kisses down her shoulder to her breast following the swirling silver runes with his lips. He found her nipple with a gentle swirl of his tongue he drew the nipple into his hot mouth and sucked hard.

Savanna arched into him with a gasp of pleasure. Her fingers found his thick hair holding him to her. She trembled at the pleasure that radiated through her. Heat burned making her pant as her skin blazed with a fire all its own.

Then moaned in shock as his hands pulled her breaches open and his hand found her moist heat bellow. She shuddered at the touch of his fingers in that so secret part of her. The ache that had been in her lower abdomen moved quickly to where his fingers flicked and her body quivered as heat and pleasure built making her hold her breath and small cry's of need burst from her throat. She never thought she could ever feel any hotter but to her surprise a blast of pure heat exploded through her making her head explode. Her mouth found his shoulder and she bit him in ecstasy as her very first orgasm slammed into her. Shudders of pleasure made sparks flash in her eyes and her mind went blank in shock. All she could do was shudder and hold onto Oran as she rode each wave that crashed through her.

Savanna moaned as her body shivered from the aftermath. The pleasure had released some of her pain but not all. She still ached within. Her hand found his member. It was hard and throbbing as she wrapped her hand around it. she knew what his member was for though she never experienced it for her-self. Now she wanted him inside her.

    Oran gasped and stiffened at her touch but he didn't stop her as she explored and learned what pleased him. He shuddered as she gripped him and brought forth his pre-fluid to run freely over her hand making his member slick. She made him moan. His body shook as he once more fought for control.

    Oran pulled away from her and she whimpered in want as she reached for him. His hands unbuckled her dagger and placed it upon the floor next to his shirt then with a swift tug he pulled her breaches off and then stood and removed his own. He stood naked before her heat filled gaze. Every muscle in his dark body tense and quivering like a bowstring. Sweat glistened on his skin making her want to taste him. The silver mark on his chest almost glowed against his darkness.

    With a low growl Oran picked her up and placed her fully upon the cot. His hot body covering hers. Then his mouth once more claimed hers but this time he didn't hold back. He devoured her leaving her breathless as he nipped and licked and dove as far into her mouth as his tongue could reach.

    In defense she thrust her tongue into his mouth and tasted him fully with her tongue and the jolts of pleasure she had gotten from him she knew she was now giving him as he suddenly growled in her mouth and pulled back just enough so that their tongues had room to war together equally.

His body gently rocked against her. A shock of electricity shot through her core at the motion. She moaned and ran her hands down his back to his heavily muscled buttocks and squeezed her fingers into his hard flesh.

Trembling with need she allowed her legs to fall open giving him access to her lower region. Her knees trembled as his member rubbed her secret place. Sweat soaked both their skins as heat blazed through them both. She could only gasp and tremble as he gently rocked against her. She could feel him tensing.

" Oran?" she could only cry as she felt both their needs burning within her. Gasping she clung to him trembling. " Oran? Please?"

" I don't want to hurt you." He moaned into her ear strain deepening his voice into a huskiness that made her belly quiver anew.

Savanna reached down seeking his member. Oran's hand followed with a curse as he tried to stop her. She was done with waiting she cried out. " Take me Oran!"

Her cry was lost with the roar that broke from deep within him. His hand gripped his member tightly and his face looked hungrily into hers almost animalistic with his need and she knew his control was gone.

That was the only warning she got. Then his

member found her opening and slid into her and a sharp pain, as he ripped unchecked through her maidenhead. Then his kiss stole her cry of pain as her body stiffened in shock. Her nails raked his back and he growled in answer to it by pumping his member in and out of her hard and fast. All she could do was hold on. The pain had gone as soon as he had entered her now pleasure like she never felt before built within her at each new thrust of his hips.

 Unsure what to do with her legs she wrapped them around his waist and soon she learned his rhythm. She matched him thrust for thrust like the war that they had done with their tongues. Her eyes opened for she had closed them when he had first entered her. She saw his face straining over her his eyes closed. His pleasure was storming through her just like in the dream/memory.

 She wanted his kiss. With her hands she grabbed his beard and brought his mouth down to hers. She felt him shudder then his mouth claimed her again in a kiss filled with animal heat. Deep he dove with his tongue and with his member until they synchronized. Thrusting into her as if starved. Sweat from both their bodies making them slick and the feel of his chest on her sensitive nipples sent her over the edge.

 She screamed into his mouth as her body exploded in a nerve ending rush of endless pleasure as her insides spasmodically griped him over and over as if milking him for his seed. Her hands pulled his beard.

Suddenly he tensed then he shuddered uncontrollably as he shouted into her mouth as his own orgasm exploded from him and slammed into her sending her swirling upon an endless sea of pleasure. His body slammed hard into her once twice thrice. With the last thrust she spiraled into another explosion of pleasure on top of all of his that wracked her body. Then he slammed into her hard for another set of three that made her explode again. Then another set that made her scream in pleasure so intense that it sent her spinning into oblivion.

Savanna became aware of a soft brushing of whiskers against her neck. It tickled and giggling she buried her hands into Oran's beard to hold it away with her fingers. He lay on top of her but his weight was on his knuckles and she found him looking deeply into her face.

" Did I hurt you?" concern wrinkled his brow making him look almost bearish in the dim light. Guilt filled his heart. *I didn't expect her to be a virgin. It must have hurt bursting through her maidenhead like that.*

Chuckling she pulled him down and kissed him as she felt the guilt that radiated from him in waves. " No."

Her legs were still wrapped around his waist and she could feel his member still deep inside her. She moved her hips and pleasure radiated through her making her moan.

The guilt vanished and with a chuckle Oran suddenly rolled over and pulled her on top of him. His gaze trailed over the Dwarvish runes that ran delicately over her skin like the most intricate silk lace his grandmother use to make. The only parts that weren't rune covered were her eyes, mouth, chin and breasts.

With a chuckle Oran wondered what they looked like on her backside. He would have flipped her over to look but finding her-self now on top gave his mate the chance to investigate him, which she did with a heated gaze and hot hands. Her white blond hair brushed his chest as she leaned over him with a wicked gleam in her eyes and her creamy olive breasts hung large and tantalizing before him.

" I think I like this." She chuckled throatily at him. Her mouth twitched in humor as she trailed her finger down his neck to his chest. With a grin she shifted her hips and heat and pleasure that swept through her from the action made her rear back with a gasp, arching her back as his hands went to her tiny waist to try and hold her from falling backwards as she found her rhythm.

Oran trembled as his member instantly awoke. Pleasure and need unfurled within him making his hips grind to meet her as she ground her hips back and forth. Sweat once more broke out upon his body as the furnace within him burst open and consumed him.

Savanna held her one hand behind her for

balance while her other one held her belly as once more need ached within her. Pleasure rose within her as she whimpered. It swirled and built making the ache in her belly worsen. She thought she was going to burst when suddenly all the painful tension inside her let go with a wave of intense pleasure that made her cry out in ecstasy.

Oran growled and bucked violently beneath her as he felt her orgasm grip and release him with every spasm. His pleasure built. Once again she shook with another orgasm bigger than the first. Tremors shook them both as she found release over and over and he felt his seed wanting to rise for a second time. ***To soon! Not yet!***

Oran tried to get on top but Savanna was not having that. With a growl she flung forward and gripped his chest with both hands and her nails bit into his skin drawing blood. She snarled at him eyes blazing as ecstasy swept through her with each thrust and grind.

Oran shouted and with a massive heave she was under him once more and he was slamming hard into her hot core, his seed riding hot and heavy deep within him.

Savanna gasped as he flipped her under him. Her mouth opened in shock as he pounded violently into her. His weight and strength held her in place. All she could do was grip his beard and hang on and grip it she did pulling on it with all her strength.

Oran went wild when Savanna grabbed his

beard and pulled. His eyes rolled back and his mouth turned into a snarl as the mixture of pain and pleasure made his seed rise fast hot and explosive. Suddenly he arched away from her almost pulling his beard from her tiny hands and his roar was almost primal as his seed and orgasm exploded inside her drowning out her scream of ecstasy.

Trembling he looked into Savannas shocked gaze.

" Oh, wow." Was all she could say for her throat had gone dry.

It was too much Oran's laughter filled the tent. He collapsed on top of her still shaking with mirth, his mouth showering her with tiny kisses.

Savanna giggled as his kisses tickled her over sensitive skin. Then to her horror her stomach growled loudly. She closed her eyes and groaned wishing it had stayed silent for just a few more minutes for she wasn't ready for him to get off her yet.

Oran chuckled sensing the conflict within her. " There is food waiting for us on the table. If we are going to continue this we need as much energy as we can get. Come, let us get some sustenance before both our belly's growl."

With a sigh of regret, she watched Oran as he got off her and stood up. His legs shook with reaction and his stomach growled to prove the truth of his words.

Savanna giggled throatily at the sound. Then her stomach growled again in answer to his. Looking down at her belly she said, " Ok you win."

Oran helped her from the cot. He steadied her as her legs wobbled. He was amazed that this tiny girl held his heart and soul in her tiny hands. She didn't even come to his chin and he was five foot eight. Finally he got his chance to see her backside as she walked unsteadily towards the table and his eyes widened in shock.

A Dwarf ring covered her back. Black runes were in-scripted into the rings edges. The ring itself was silver like the runes on her face and torso and the silver runes that flowed around her hips, sides and shoulders made a frame around the ring. What the runes meant he didn't know for only the Holy ones could read them. No longer would she have to worry about acceptance into the Holt for the runes spoke of her acceptance by the Dwarves Gods. He saw the colored marks of all seven gods filling the inside of the ring.

Shaken, Oran followed her. His eyes thoughtful as he joined her at the table. What Savanna had done by binding her-self to him worried him. No female had ever bound them-selves to a male before. If he should die in battle she would not be able to breed with another male.

Oran knew they both would have to return to the Holt. The Holy Ones needed to see her and make sense of the runes. His father and mother needed to meet his mate and a choice would have to be made.

CHAPTER TEN

The entire Thirteenth Company had been shocked when Oran took Savanna as his mate but to find her covered by Dwarven runes the next day had many looking at her with mixed emotions. Eyes followed her everywhere she went.

Plans were being made for a journey back to the Holt. The decision on who was to leave came down to four of Savanna's uncles her brother Braun and Oran and Savanna her-self. They would be leaving in four days time.

Savanna sat in Braun's tent as her uncles wrote out the supplies they would need for the three-week trip to the Holt. Her eyes watching everything that went on around her with interest. Mostly she watched Oran. He looked delicious in his russet leathers and chain. Every muscle in his body rippled as he paced before her. He was the only russet warrior in the tent the others wore silver and black armor.

It had taken them three days to decide on who was going and who was going to replace the ones leaving. In those three days her standing among the Dwarves had shifted radically. Where the warriors had once ignored her, she was now watched with speculating eyes and greeted with tentative smiles and nods.

Only her four uncles, Braun, and Gavan had been shown the ring upon her back. That had been the day Oran had announced their return to the Holt and for warriors to travel with them to keep her safe on the journey there.

  The black shirt and breaches hid most of her runes from wondering eyes but the ones on her hands, face and neck brought speculating stares from all who looked at her. This made her feel uncomfortable when walking around outside with all staring at her. It took her uncles and Braun to convince her that the runes made her look beautiful not ugly.

  During the day she could be found healing the wounded or hiding in a tent for she couldn't bare the stares from the warriors around her. Her nights she spent in Oran's arms. Their love making sometimes gentle but mostly wild and full of passion. It was Oran who kissed her tears when the stares got to bad.

  Now she sat as Oran paced back and forth in front of her. Worry lined his face. She ached to wipe the worry from him but with all her uncles and brother present she didn't dare. So she sat silently as the discussion around her grew into arguments over what route should be taken..

  The only thing they did agree on was the weather. Winter was around the corner here but up in the mountains snow already lay heavy upon it. Snowstorms raged almost every day up among the peaks while here they got chilling rain and sleet. Winter gear was a must for this journey as well as winter tents.

  " Oran!" Braun growled annoyed. " Sit down before you dig a trench to deep to get out of. Besides you're upsetting my sister with your worrying."

Contrite Oran looked at Savanna who sat white and taut in her chair. Her hands were clenching and unclenching in her lap, eyes widely watching him.

With a sigh he knelt in front of her and took her chilled hands into his warm ones. " You're cold."

He gently rubbed his warmth into her fingers. Now his worry was focused upon her. A nod from Braun and he went to the cot and pulled Braun's coverings off and proceeded to wrap her in them to keep her warm.

Savanna couldn't resist. She wrapped her cold fingers into his warm beard and pulled his lips to hers for a hot kiss. Instantly his heat filled her taking the chill from her.

" Mmmm." She sighed. " That's better. Feel warmer already."

Chuckles broke out around her from her male relatives. They had already told both of them that they all approved of their bonding though they still wondered about her bonding to Oran. Sadness had filled their eyes at the consequences for she could never re-mate if he died. Loaded with that knowledge her uncles had spoken to Oran about staying in the Holt with her and never go out to battle again whilst she lived.

" You play with fire.." Oran began with a low growl.

" You'll get burned." Savanna chuckled as she finished the well-known saying. Her eyes danced in mirth as she looked hungrily into his eyes. " It was the fastest way I could think of to get warm."

Her uncle Garn snickered at her sally and Moag snorted.

" Braun get that brazier going so the girl can get warm." Garth growled in consternation, his annoyance flashing in his eyes. " Or we won't get nothing done with these two flirting around us."

They all roared in laughter as Braun chuckled and went to start the brazier. Once it was going the heat from it quickly filled the small tent. He re-joined the group at his table where maps and lists were spread all over it along with empty cups.

" I think we should take this route." Garn pointed out following it with his finger. " It will take us closer to the mountain but it is shorter than this route that Garth wants to take. It will shave a couple days off our trip."

" But we have no idea how much snow blocks it at this spot." Beldin pointed at the spot he mentioned. Worry lined his face. " If its blocked it's going to take us more time to either clear it if its not that deep or to go back to find another way through."

Once again all four of Savanna's uncles started to argue. There voices rising as tempers flared.

Savanna huddled deeper into her blanket. Her blood felt like ice within her as she shivered uncontrollably. Every time they got angry she got cold. Her eyes unfocused and her head started to spin dizzily. Suddenly her stomach clenched and pain filled her. She couldn't take it any longer.

" Enough!" Savanna had no idea how she came to be standing. She couldn't remember leaving her chair. Her body shook with cold. " Chose a path!"

All of them looked at her in shock their mouths open in surprise at her out burst. She had no idea that she had spoken to them in Dwarf and that her eyes blazed with icy fire.

Oran pulled her into his arms as she began to cry. Icy tears running down her chilled face. She was shivering so hard her teeth chattered.

" Easy." Oran murmured into her ear as he suddenly swept her up into his arms and took her to the cot to sit there with her in his arms. He looked at the others concern filling his voice. " She's like ice!"

Savanna buried her face into his beard her fingers clutching the blankets. Chills swept through her making her shiver and shuddering gasps burst from her in small cries. She couldn't stop her tears as they fell streaming from her wide eyes. All she could do was stare helplessly at them as she sobbed.

Instantly her uncles surrounded them. She felt them touch her face with their hot hands. Curses filled the air around her as everyone scrambled to get her warm.

" When did you learn Dwarf?" Braun asked her when he held a cup of hot tea to her lips and she sipped the hot fluid gratefully but it didn't touch the ice deep within her.

" The morning after I bit Oran." She told him

around her shivering lips.

Her uncles grunted at her words as Braun chuckled amused. " devious of you to keep it secret."

" She's Dwarf alright." Moag snorted.

Oran sat with her on the cot trying to rub warmth back into her shivering body. His concern for her swept through the ice. She looked up at him with pleading eyes.

" So cold." She whimpered. Her eyes pleading for him to help her.

Oran kissed her brow. His lips boiling compared to the chill of her skin. The heat from his kiss swept fire through the ice and she screamed in pain at its passing. She gasped and shuddered in shock as the pain intensified. As suddenly as it appeared the cold and pain were gone. Leaving her weak and trembling in Oran's arms.

Slowly heat once more filled her.

" What happened Savanna?" Oran asked her gently as he continued to place kisses upon her now warming brow.

" So much anger." She cried softly into his beard. " It was consuming me. Filling me with its chill."

" Whose anger?" Braun asked as he crouched down next to her. His eyes watching her closely as their uncles hovered in the background.

" Everyone's." she looked at him with pain filled eyes. " I felt everyone's anger and it chilled everything inside me."

" You felt all of our emotions?" Braun asked in surprise then looked at Oran. " She needs to get to my mother. The sooner the better. Her gifts have gotten stronger if she can now feel all of us. Can you imagine what would happen if she were caught in a battle?"

" We need to control ourselves when we are near her." Oran said at the same time as he glared warningly at her uncles even as he kissed her brow sending more warmth sweeping through her.

" We will take Garn's route." Beldin announced. He glared at Garth when he opened his mouth to argue. " It is the fastest route even if it's blocked. We will take five more warriors with us just incase. Five extra hands digging will go faster than just us six." He looked down at Savanna. " Sorry lass but you will not dig one spoonful of snow if I have anything to say about it."

Savanna nodded to let him know she understood. Hunger made her stomach growl and she blushed as everyone heard it.

" I'll go get some food." Moag chuckled as he headed towards the entrance.

" I'll go with you and help bring back enough for everyone." Beldin said as he followed him from the tent.

Savanna now able to hold her cup of tea drank the last of it and handed it over to Braun who re-filled it and handed it back to her. She sipped the hot liquid as she tried to shrug out of the covers as she began to sweat from the heat that filled her.

Oran chuckled as he gently unwrapped her for she was trying to not spill her tea all over them. " Give Braun your tea and we can deal with these annoying covers."

Savanna giggled as she handed her brother her cup. With Oran's help the covers were extracted from around her and instantly she felt cooler. She took back her cup and took another sip as she leaned into Oran's hard chest. His metal chain mail filled her with its soothing smell.

" Now that we got that settled." Garn growled his eyes twinkling, " Lets decide who the other five are going to be."

Moag and Beldin returned with trays loaded with food just in time to here the names of the extra five that had been chosen to go with them.

Moag placed his tray on the cot close enough so both Savanna and Oran could reach the food and chuckled when Oran proceeded to feed her from his fingers while she giggled.

Beldin placed his on the table covering the papers that still lay upon its surface ignoring the growls from Garn and Garth as he did so.

" Braun go let them know they are going with us and why. Don't tell them anything about the girl." Garth said as he pulled his supply list from beneath the tray. His brow wrinkled even more as he scanned the list once more to see if he had missed anything. " I feel we are missing something but can't think what it could be. Here you look and see if you see anything missing?" he said as he handed it to Garn.

Garn took the list in one hand and a chicken leg in the other. He ripped a piece of meat off with his teeth as he scanned the list. Handing it back he said with a chuckle, " You forgot the braziers and the bedding."

" Ah it seems I did." Garth chuckled as he wrote those onto his list. He then put the list down and helped him-self to a leg as well. Still chuckling as he grabbed a second piece of chicken with his other.

Savanna ate what Oran fed her. The chicken she found a little to greasy for her liking had refused to eat any when he offered it to her so he fed her bread and cheese instead.

They cleaned the tray of most of the food when Braun returned with five more Dwarves. They nodded to her when they entered then stood waiting by the entrance for the tent wasn't big enough for all of them.

" We will leave as soon as our supplies are gathered. You five get our supplies. Braun and Moag see about getting us ponies from the hostler. Garth and I will see about food for the trip." Garn handed a copy of the list to each group. " Oran find Savanna more clothing for a winter travel through the mountains. I don't want my niece freezing on the way to the Holt."

Oran grinned down at Savanna. " Well I got my order to fill. Would you like to come with me?"

Savanna grinned back with a twinkle in her eye, " I'd better go with you. That way I can be there to make sure the clothes fit."

Together they left the tent and went in search of the supply wagon.

CHAPTER ELEVEN

Savanna had never ridden a horse much less the pony that Oran proceeded to place her upon two days later. She looked down at him with large frightened eyes. " I don't know how to ride."

Oran grinned up at her, " Good time to learn."

" What do I do?" she asked as he mounted his pony.

" Just hang on." Oran chuckled at her as he swung his pony around to come up next to her. " Grip the pony's sides with your knees. He will follow the others once we get moving."

The pony shook his head making her gasp at the motion. He shifted his weight to one side and Savanna gripped the reins tightly. Nervously she looked at her pony. " Will he buck me off?"

" No he won't" Oran chuckled next to her. " He's the gentlest of the bunch. Now Rider here would buck if you tried to ride him for he's mine. Only I can ride him."

Savanna looked at Rider with wide eyes. He was a dappled gray color with a dark mane and tail. She found him beautiful. *I think I like ponies. They aren't as far from the ground as horses and they are quieter and Rider does look beautiful with that dark mane and tail.*

Rider arched his neck and tail and did a little hop his head turned to look at her as if he heard her.

Savanna then looked down at her pony. He was

a golden color with white mane and tail. *Oran had said he's a palomino. He looks peachy colored to me and he glows lovely in the sunshine. I hope he doesn't buck. I've never ridden before and I only hope I don't fall off. I wonder if the bit in his mouth hurts him when I pull on the reins. It would annoy me if I had that bit in my mouth and had some fool person yanking on it. I'll just have to be careful not to yank to hard. I don't want to hurt him.*

" Does any of his tack hurt him?" she turned to look questioning at Oran.

" No." Oran grinned, " Unless someone puts it on him wrong then it will."

Savanna looked down at her pony thoughtfully. " I guess I need to learn how to put your equipment on so I don't hurt you by doing it wrong."

Oran chuckled softly, " I will teach you how to care for your pony Savanna. Your packs hold all his cleaning supplies and I will show you how to use them when we camp tonight."

Savanna smiled gratefully into Oran's eyes. " I think I'd like that."

" His name is Sunny." Braun told her as he rode his pony a black with two white stockings on her other side. Looking at Oran he said, " We're just about ready to head out. Just waiting for the final pack pony to be loaded."

Holding the reins in her left hand Savanna pulled her heavy cloak around her to keep the chill wind off her neck. Oran had braided her hair before leaving the tent so that it hung thickly down her back and out of her face. Now she wished it hung loosely for it would have kept her warm instead she had to pull the hood of her cloak around her face to stay warm.

" Okay, lets get moving!" Garth barked as he rode past with the final pony loaded down with their packs following on a lead. " Want to get to our planned camp before dark."

Savanna held on as her pony went into a walk following the others. *Well this isn't too bad.* She thought until the ones in front broke into a trot as soon as they hit the edge of the encampment and her pony did the same and she started to bounce all over the place. Instinctively she gripped the pony with her knees to hold on gritting her teeth as her bottom slapped painfully into the saddle as she tried to keep from falling off. *This mustn't be comfortable for either of us!*

Sunny seemed to agree for he looked back at her with an indignant eye.

Savanna closed her eyes and felt the rhythm of the pony. *Must find a way to move with him so it's easier on both of us.* A blush suffused her cheeks as she remembered when she had ridden Oran that first night. *Could it be that simple?* Without thinking about it she did it. using her knees to lift her and lower her to match the gait of the pony beneath her. To her surprise it worked. She was moving with the pony not perfectly like the others but enough that she was no longer hurting her-self or the pony beneath her.

Sunny seemed to sigh at her as she struggled to maintain the rhythm but her legs started to burn after a few minutes and she would lose the rhythm completely only to gain it again when her legs cooled.

" It'll get easier the more you ride him." Oran said grinning at her. " You sure figured out how to find his rhythm in this gait faster than I thought you would. We will go into a faster gait soon and that one will be easier than the trot."

Savanna was so busy concentrating on matching the pony and not falling off that she just nodded to let him know she understood him, she had to open her cloak for she was now sweating from the exertion of riding. Her bottom grew numb and her legs hurt the longer they rode.

Suddenly the gait changed. They were going faster and the pony's gait smoothed out enough for her to rest in the saddle. *I like this gait better*. Her pony seemed to agree for he arched his neck and tail with ears pointed straight ahead. Her legs still burned but at least her bottom was no longer painfully slapping into the saddle.

Sunny whickered as if in agreement.

The road they traveled on wound through forest so thick that the empty branches of the trees stretched across the road like a tunnel. Every little while they slowed to a walk to rest the ponies. Savanna and Sunny both looked forward to the walks. She would run her fingers over Sunny's sweating shoulders in wonder for her fear of riding was gone.

Savanna took in the others as she now rode without the need to concentrate. Once more Oran stood out among the Dwarves. Oran's the only russet colored armor bright against the silver and black of her kin and the dark brown of the five new ones. *I wonder what the color of their armor means?*

" Is there meaning behind the color of each warriors armor?" she asked Oran as they rode side by side for the entire company was going in twos on the road.

Oran smiled, " yes there is." He grinned broadly as he nodded towards Braun and her uncles. " The black and silver are for the blood of Garon the first of their line. The dark brown of the others are for the line of Dagon and my russet for the line of Magog. There are two more colors that you haven't seen yet. The white of Rogan and the blue of Chan stay within the Holt. They guard the Holt at all times."

Savanna nodded to let him know she understood. " Who are they the ones of each line?"

" They are brothers. Their father comes from the line of Aaron in the Cobalt Mountains in the east mountain range. When the Holt grows too big five of the main line of each blood leave with their families and form another Holt in a mountain range close by." He told her.

" How many Holts are there?" she asked as her pony sidled closer to his.

" Fourteen." He told her with humor sparkling

in his eyes.

At midday they stopped and ate some meat and cheese with biscuits as they walked around to stretch their legs. Then back up onto the ponies they went heading into that dreaded trot that Savanna and Sunny both hated then into the low canter that was bliss for both as the group headed north.

The sun was starting to go down and Savanna fought to keep her eyes open but they kept closing and her head would nod waking her up. They had slowed to a walk and that was when she fell asleep riding Sunny. The reins falling from her slack fingers to trail on the ground making Sunny come to a complete stop.

With a chuckle and a wink at Braun, Oran gently scooped the girl into his lap as Braun took up Sunny's reins. Braun pulled a blanket from one of the packs on Sunny and helped Oran cover her with it as she started to lightly snore. Then they all walked on.

They reached their destination just as the sun began to sink behind the mountain bathing the land in a soft red glow the forest starting to give way to the mountain terrain around them.

Oran waited for Braun to dismount before handing over the sleeping girl. Once she was safely in his arms did he also dismount and hand the reins over to Tobin who smiled wryly as he led his gray and their three ponies to the hidden stable. Corbin and Darn followed with the rest after Garth and Garn took two packs from one of the ponies.

They strode into the hidden cave. Not many

knew it was there for the Dwarves knew how to keep their caves secret and this cave was well hidden from the road. Only a fellow Dwarf would have known it was there.

Garth and Garn each had a lit brazier and were already preparing tea and supper over them while Moag and Beldin threw down the bedrolls.

" Put her here." Moag grunted when he finished unrolling one of the beds then he motioned Braun to lay the girl down. " She did good for her first day of rough travel."

They left Savanna sleeping on the bed. Oran had removed her dagger and placed it next to her then kissed her brow before joining the others who had gathered around the brazier with the tea.

Garn handed him a cup as his eyes contemplated the sleeping girl. He wondered what other gifts might awaken inside her before the journey ended.

" Ponies are all settled." Tobin said when he entered the cave. " My brothers Corbin and Darn are standing guard over them and my cousins Brok and Kalin are guarding the perimeter. " He rolled out his bedding and then hunched down by the brazier. " Who will stand second watch with me?"

" I will." Braun told him as he sipped his tea. " Pony watch or perimeter?"

" Perimeter." Tobin answered amber eyes thoughtful. " Who wants Pony watch?"

Garn handed a cup to Tobin and the Dwarf looked up at him as he took it with gratefulness in his amber eyes. " So you are of the blood of Hagin?"

Beldin lifted his tea to Tobin at the same time. " Moag and I can watch the Ponies."

Tobin looked startled. " Yes he's my father. How did you know?"

" Your eyes. His are the same shade," Garn smiled, " and you have his features."

Tobin grinned, "My twin is at the Holt with mother and my three sisters." He chuckled, " father gave all of us his eyes. Mother wasn't pleased about that. She wanted the girls to have dark eyes like her."

Garn laughed. " I know your mother lad for she's my sister."

" Then we are cross related." Tobin smiled at him from across the brazier. Then shock darkened his eyes as he looked over at the sleeping girl. " She is your Niece?"

Garn nodded but said nothing letting the lad put things together for him-self. He wasn't disappointed.

" I am cross related to her as well." Tobin breathed surprised then stood up. " I need to go let the others know of who will be replacing them. Thank you for the tea."

They all watched him leave the cave his eyes deep in thought.

Savanna woke with a start. Her internal alarm was screaming at her making her shiver in panic. Darkness surrounded her and she didn't know where she was. Shaking her heart beating wildly in her chest she sat up her hand going to her thigh only to find her dagger gone. Frantically she swept her hand around her in search for it and found Oran's shoulder in the dark. She gripped him tightly and shook him.

"What?" Oran growled sleepily at her from the darkness next to her.

"Danger!" She hissed at him terrified. "Where's my dagger!"

Instantly Oran was wide-awake. He could feel the girl trembling next to him.

"Garn! Garth! Everyone! Wake up!" he hissed.

Instantly the sound of shuffling filled the darkness then a flash as a brazier was lit. The light filled the cave as everyone looked at Oran with weapons in hand. They were all standing prepared for battle.

Savanna saw her dagger and grabbed it. She unsheathed it and looked at the entrance. Her eyes wide in panic. She could feel danger close by.

"It's close!" she hissed. Her body had stopped trembling when she had her dagger safely to hand. She tensed gripping the dagger with both hands like a sword.

All eyes were looking at her now. She could feel all their mixed emotions swirling inside her with a flood of heat and ice. Alarm shouted within her and she snarled in answer.

"To arms!" came shouted from outside as

howls of rage and pain filled the air.

Braun entered the cave yelling. " Drake!"

Everyone ran out of the cave.

Moonlight bathed the scene of battle as the Dwarves rushed the large animal that roared in pain and rage as the Dwarves attacked it. Swords and axes bit into its body opening its flesh with large gapping wounds that bled black blood as the Dwarves fought it with battle cries. Its eyes glowed with a sickly yellow light as it swatted two Dwarves out of its path and bit another with its fanged mouth. The sound of breaking bone mingled with the scream of pain from the Dwarf filled the air.

Savanna felt their pain and screamed. She almost dropped her dagger as the shock of it went through her as if it had been her who had been bit and swatted and with that pain came a blast of icy rage that roared through her. She looked at the beast attacking them. Never had she seen anything like it. The thing towered over the Dwarves. Hide glistening whitely in the moonlight as its serpent like body twisted around to slice huge claws across Oran's chest as he tried to take its head with his axe. He staggered from the blow but stayed on his feet as he made another swing his axe flashing in the moonlight.

The Drake roared as the axe bit into its shoulder spraying thick black blood everywhere. It turned and grasped Oran in its jaws and shook him then flung him into a tree.

Oran lay lifeless upon the ground his axe had landed a few feet from his hand. The Drake moved to finish him off.

Savanna screamed in pain and rage as she attacked standing over Oran as he lay still beneath her. She didn't remember moving. Her dagger sliced into cold scales like butter as she slashed its nose. Fire blazed all along the blade going into the creature making it shrill in shocked pain and fear. It swung to hit her and she danced under its claws and once more sliced her dagger across the flesh of the drakes shoulder making it scream. Its head came around to bite her and she brought her dagger around in a curving arch slicing into the flesh under its jaws spraying blood all over her and the ground.

The Dwarves swarmed over it as it thrashed and screamed its death cries as their axes finished it off.

Savanna crouched over Oran as she placed her hand upon his bleeding chest. Ice roared through her blood making her shiver. She was aware of everything around her. Every eye upon her. Every wound. Every shallow breath Oran took.

The Dwarves stared at her in shocked surprise as her power blasted through them all.

CHAPTER TWELVE

Savanna sat silently in the cave as the Dwarves cleaned up the carcass of the drake outside. She stared into the flames of the brazier as she waited for the tea to finish brewing. Moag had told her she would only get in the way but she knew it was because they were afraid of her. *Hell I'm afraid of my-self.*

Savanna looked over at the four Dwarves lying on the beds. They were still out even though she had healed them. *I healed them all while touching Oran. My gift is getting stronger. What I did to that drake scares me. If I can do that to a drake what can I do to people? Can I hurt people?*

Her mind veered from a memory of the last village she had been in. *That was in self-defense.* But a niggling doubt whispered *was it?*

Savanna tried not thinking about the battle but her mind swept over it in detail. Hers had not been the final blow that killed it but she had sliced it with her dagger without hesitation. *If I had not acted these four would be dead instead of sleeping.*

She shook at the thought of losing Oran and her blood froze at the thought. Once more she went to him and gently touched his face. *Why won't you wake?*

Savanna ran her trembling fingers over the slices in his armor. She could feel the metal warm beneath her tips. In her mind she saw the metal mend as she healed the tears beneath her fingers as she would a wound. The chain melting and blending to once more reform into links to become whole beneath her fingers.

Only his leathers bore the marks of the Drakes claws and fangs for she had no gift for them. Her hand strayed to her dagger. She had made it with only her hands and mind. The stone she had felt in a huge rock and had called it forth. Then she had molded the two metals together forming the blade into the shape she wanted. The handle was also made from the two metals. Into the hilt she fused the stone making the dagger whole. *I know longer care. I will not hide my gifts any longer.*

Tears made her eyes bright as she once more touched his face and then kissed his brow before going to the one laying closest to her. She looked down at the sleeping Dwarf.

He wore the dark brown armor that she now knew was the line of Dagon. His chain mail had been truly ravaged for the beast had bitten him upon his shoulder. She knelt at his side and with her fingers healed the chain melting and reweaving the links into new ones as some had vanished into the Drakes mouth. Done she went to the other two and did the same.

Tired she sighed and went to see if the tea was ready. Seeing that it was she poured her-self a cup and slowly sipped it as her eyes watched the entrance.

She could feel the fear coming from those outside and knew they were just on the other side of the entrance. Her tears flowed to feel their fear of her.

It was just like the villagers. Closing her eyes against her sorrow and pain she tried to hold back the sobs that were swelling painfully into her chest.

Suddenly arms were around her holding her tightly as words of comfort were spoken into her hair, it was too much, Savanna burst into heart rending sobs into Braun's chest. From the shuffling of feet she knew the others had come in as well to gather uncomfortably around them but she didn't care.

" Why won't they wake?" She sobbed. " I healed them but still they lay unmoving."

" Shhhh." Braun soothed and told her gently. " They will wake when they are ready."

Savanna pulled away from him sniffling and wiped her eyes on her sleeve. " There's something you should know." She looked up at Braun with red-rimmed eyes. " I can't keep this secret any longer. I've had this gift since I found my twin."

Savanna placed her hand upon Braun's silver chain mail where one of the Drakes claws had ripped it then pleaded. " Please don't fear me."

With those words she healed the metal before all their shocked eyes. The metal melting and moving to reform into whole links the slice gone.

Done she reached down and pulled out her dagger and held it up for all to see. " I made this from a chunk of steel and silver. The stone I called forth from a huge bolder where I had found my twin. In my grief and anger I forged this with my hands and mind and nothing else."

Garth took the dagger from her to examine it closely. His fingers touched every inch with a critical eye. " This is of master craftsmanship. Unflawed in any way and is of one piece even with the stone. Truly a work of art."

He handed it to the others to go over it as his eyes looked down at his niece with contemplation. " Any other gifts that we should know about?"

" I'll let you know if any should crop up." Savanna told him. " but that's all I know of at the moment and that I can sense danger when it's close." She shrugged her shoulders, " If you want to call that a gift. It has kept me alive this far. Though this is the first time I had to use my dagger in battle. I usually run when my alarm system sounds."

Garn snorted. " Our females don't fight. We would rather they run than stand and do battle. You felt our fear and knew it was for you but you thought it was of your gifts. Well lass you're wrong."

His eyes held her transfixed. " we feared for your safety. You see we all have some form of gift. We are born with them. Garth has gift over metal just like you. I have the gift of extracting precious stones from rock. " He chuckled at her look of surprise. " yes just like you. So far the gifts you're displaying are all Dwarven gifts. Only you have more than one gift."

" How many gifts are there?" she asked as she snuffled, her nose running from her crying.

A Dwarf in brown armor chuckled and handed her a handkerchief so she could blow her nose. Which she did loudly. Blushing she started to hand it back but the Dwarf whose handkerchief it was shook his head. " Keep it. I have more and besides I feel you're going to be needing it before this journey ends."

Garn chuckled. " there are many minor gifts such as blood mages like your brother Braun and his mother. They can read bloodlines. The gift to read rock, to know if it's flawed or strong those who have it are trained to dig through the mountain to find mines and places to live and if their gift is strong they are trained to handle precious stones. Those with the gift to call precious stones from rock are trained in mining. Then there are the ones who have the gift over metals. Most have one metal they are attuned to while very few are attuned to two and its extremely rare to be attuned to them all. They are trained in the smithy as crafters of weapons, armor and sometimes jewelry. The gift of healing belongs to the Holy ones. They also have the gift to read runes like the ones on your skin."

Savanna looked down at her hands. Her runes shone in the firelight. I wish I could see them all like everyone else can. It would be nice to know what they looked like.

A moan from one of the sleeping Dwarves behind her had her on her feet and at their side just as his amber eyes opened to look up at her in confusion.

"What happened?" He croaked up at her. He was one of the two that the drake had thrown at the beginning of the battle. " How did I get here?"

Savanna touched his face with trembling fingers. " You were brought in by Braun after the battle. I healed your wounds."

" Oh. " His eyes widened as his memory clicked in. " I guess it was foolish of me to rush in like that."

" Damn right!" Garth growled as he came to stand beside Savanna. His dark eyes glared down at the injured Dwarf. " If you ever do that again Tobin I will swat you my-self!"

Rebuked Tobin nodded as he looked up at him. " Yes sir!"

Savanna got up to get Tobin a cup of tea while he sat up in his bed. He smiled up at her when he took it from her. Then she went to check on the other three who still slept worry on her face. Finding them still sleeping she sighed and joined the others at the fire sitting next to Braun who handed a steaming cup out to her.

" Thanks." She smiled at him.

" Any change?" Braun asked as he sipped his own tea.

Savanna shook her head. " No they still sleep. I'm worried. They should have woken up by now."

Braun patted her hand. " Don't worry Savanna they will wake."

" Lets continue with our conversation before Tobin interrupted us." Garn chuckled as he sent a wink her way making her smile.

" Is there any gifts that all Dwarves have?" she

asked as she sipped her tea. She was fascinated that there were so many gifts and wanted to learn all she could about them.

" All Dwarves have the gift of path finding." Garn grinned. " We always know where we've been."

" Oh." Savanna said in surprise then said dryly. " Well that explains a lot."

They all laughed at her chagrined expression.

" Well we went through most of the minor gifts now lets get into the more complicated gifts." Garn chuckled his eyes twinkling at her from the other side of the fire. " Gate masters have the gift of stone and the gift of runes. The Holy ones train them though they are not a part of them. They can build hidden gates as well as find old ones that have been lost over time. These gates are used in defense of the Holt. Through these gates we can either fight or flee or hide our greatest treasure."

He took a sip of tea before continuing. " Now weapon mages are also trained by the Holy ones. They have the gift of metal and the gift of runes. With those gifts they make our greatest weapons like Oran's axe. The edge will never go dull and it will never break and nothing can stand before it for it will even slice through onyx."

Savanna looked at Oran's axe with new eyes. It was next to Oran's sleeping hand.

" Jewel mages do the same thing only with precious stones. These stones are used in jewelry. Mostly luck or protection charms are put into them, but some are used as mage focuses." Garn looked deeply at Savanna then down at the stone in the hilt of her dagger. " When you attacked the Drake defending Oran, did you know that your stone blazed with fire?"

The Dwarves looked at her expectantly. Their faces full of encouragement and with something akin to wonder.

Savanna swallowed hard as they watched her. They needed an answer so she gave them the truth. " Yes I knew. It blazed once before."

Shaking she took a sip of tea to moisten her mouth for it had gone dry with fear. She smiled shakily at Braun when he held her hand. His eyes telling her that he knew and he had seen it in her blood. " Just before I joined the Company I had finished up at the temple. It was mid of night and so tired from healing that even my alarm didn't go off to let me know He was there."

Trembling she took another sip of tea. " The arrow missed me by mere inches. I could feel the wind from its passage as it passed my cheek. I panicked. My dagger was in my hand and I threw it into the darkness from where the arrow came. The stone blazed and I could feel it for it was seeking the one who shot at me."

Savanna stared into the flames eyes haunted. " It found him." A strangled sob broke from her chest as she looked up at them with tear filled eyes. " I had run from them for so long always one step ahead. My alarm always warning me in time to run."

" But not this time." Garn sighed at her with sadness in his eyes. " What happened Savanna?"

" The dagger sank to the hilt in his chest." She shook at the memory and Braun had to take her cup with one hand as the other went around her shivering body. " It burst into flames and the man screamed. He screamed so horribly and he tried to pull it out but he couldn't. He burst into flame! I could feel the dagger! I felt its hunger as it consumed him from the inside! Then it was over. The dagger flew back to me from the darkness to land in my hand."

She sobbed brokenly as they looked at her in silence. Only her sobs and the crackling fire filled the cave. The memory of what she had done breaking her into little pieces.

" He was hunting you. So you hunted him in turn." Oran's voice sounded down at her as he suddenly sat next to her. " I have used my axe in the same manner when I invoke it. I too can feel my axes hunger for blood when it seeks the one I throw it at. It's unsettling."

Savanna turned into his embrace as she sobbed in both relief that he was ok and in reaction from her retelling. " The worst thing is that I hungered with it."

Suddenly Oran laughed. " Blood lust hits all warriors. I even succumb to it in battle especially when my axe is awakened."

" All Dwarves do." Garth growled his voice full of emotion then said with a meaningful look at Oran " Even females experience it when they defend their loved ones."

Savanna looked up at Oran seeing the weariness in his face. She wrapped her fingers into his beard and pulled him down for a gentle kiss. Trying to tell him without words how glad she was that he was ok.

" So Braun is right." Garn chuckled as he looked meaningfully at his nephew. " You need to get into the hands of his mother and into training with the Holy ones. From what you have told us not only are you a healer but also a weapon mage and a jewel mage and that my dear is a dangerous combo."

Savanna yawned and blinked her eyes at them. " Is there somewhere to bathe or do I have to wait to get all this blood off me?"

Oran looked down at her blood-covered shirt and laughed softly into her hair. " There's a hot spring next to the stable. We'll go there now." Then looked up at the others. " Unless some of you are going there?"

The others chuckled and shook their heads.
" We can wait until you're done." Braun laughed then said as Savanna yawned again. " Go before she falls asleep."

Oran went to the packs and took out fresh clothing for both of them. He also grabbed her comb and two bath towels before taking Savanna's hand and leading her from the cave.

Savanna followed Oran as he led her around an outcropping of large boulders. Trees and vines screened the large enclosure that housed the ponies. Moag and another Dwarf greeted them as they passed with knowing grins on their faces.

Savanna blushed but smiled shyly at her uncle. Then they vanished from sight as Oran took her into a stone tunnel behind the enclosure. His hand guided her for he knew the way even in the dark.

The tunnel twisted and turned until it opened up into a well-lit chamber. Stonewalls glowed with an inner light making Savanna gasp in surprised wonder. A large pool steamed in the center and she remembered his dream/memory of the other chamber that held a similar pool and stopped dead in her tracks.

" Are you sure it's safe?" she whispered up at Oran who was looking at her with concern.

Oran smiled. " It's very safe. Moag and Garn checked earlier to make sure nothing had taken residence while we were gone."

Her alarms weren't going off so she sighed and started to shed her blood soaked shirt. She put her dagger next to the edge of the pool next to his axe before pulling off her breaches. A smile played at the corners of her mouth as she saw Oran watching her every move as he striped out of his clothes. Heat burned in the depths of his eyes and he stood naked before her hungry gaze.

Savanna felt his arousal just as hers awakened within her. It blazed hot and uncontrolled within her. She slowly walked naked towards him hips swayed seductively as she neared him. She looked up into his face as her hands grabbed his black beard and was going to pull him gently but something within her suddenly didn't want to be gentle.

Savanna snarled and pulled viciously on his beard to bring his lips to her open mouth.

Oran growled savagely as the pain made his blood come instantly awake with a roar of molten heat. His arousal roared through him and his member instantly hardened. His hands gripped her waist and he picked her up and slammed her hard against the stone of the chamber wall. His mouth devoured hers just as she wrapped her legs around his hard waist. Her hands left his beard and buried themselves into his long hair gripping him to her. She snarled savagely into his mouth as her hips ground against him. His member found her entrance and slid violently into her moist hot core. His mouth swallowed her cry of pleasure. Her orgasm powerfully clenched his hard member violently.

Savanna was lost to the raging emotions filling her. Her orgasm was instant sending her over the edge of reason and into instinct as she clung to him. The stone was cool compared to the heat from their bodies and her breaths came in gasps as she raged over the edge again when he slammed into her hard and fast. His growls filling her mouth even as his tongue devoured her. His body was rock hard against hers his chest rubbing his hairs against her extremely sensitive nipples sending her crashing into a more powerful orgasm.

She gripped him as he lost control. His mouth found her sensitive spot at the base of her throat and sucked hard sending her gasping and trembling for more as his hips rocked hard against her sending his member even deeper within her as her core shook with endless spasms of pleasure.

Oran took her from the wall and lowered her to the stone floor. His mouth found her breast and sucked her hard nipple deeply into his mouth. Her cries of pleasure making him growl and pump hard into her. His member swelled as his seed rose with each thrust. He sucked her breast swirling his hot tongue around the nipple only to suck hard again sending her spinning into ecstasy.

" Oran!" Savanna cried her breath coming in swift gasps as her orgasm slammed through her in endless pleasure. She griped his hair with her hands wanting. " Oran!"

Her nails raked his back in ecstasy as her hips lifted to meet his final thrust sending them both over the edge

Oran didn't hear her for his head roared with the rising of his own orgasm. His seed rising hot and fast. He was lost to the need to spill his hot seed deep within her quivering belly. Then it came the hot liquid spilling from him in molten pleasure so powerful his vision blurred and his head exploded with sparks that danced before his eyes.

Savanna screamed as his seed and pleasure exploded into her sending her crashing even higher than before. Again. And Again.

Savanna lay trembling beneath him her skin hypersensitive to every touch. Even the air sent her shivering with delight. Spasms of pleasure still swept through her. Her fingers relaxed against his back. She felt stickiness on her fingers.

Savanna stared at her fingers in confusion for they were covered in blood. Shaking she said. " Oran?"

Oran lay heavy upon her. He heard her calling to him but he couldn't move for she felt too good to let go so all he did was moan in answer.

"Oran! Oran you're bleeding." Savanna sobbed. " What have I done to you?"

Oran looked at her as he lifted him-self on his hands to look down at her then began to shake with laughter. " You drew my blood with your nails. Savanna, please don't cry. I needed to feel pain for my seed to rise. It is necessary."

Savanna looked at him with horror and guilt. Her tears rolling down her cheeks as she sobbed holding her blood covered hands up for him to see. " How is this necessary?"

CHAPTER THIRTEEN

It took Oran almost half an hour to calm Savanna. His eyes filled with amusement as her face went from shocked horror to chagrin then to weak chuckles as he explained the mating behaviors of males and females. He found her blushes endearing to watch. *She's so innocent when it comes to the joining of males and females that it leaves me to wonder how she survived within the Company with all the hot-blooded males around her and still remain innocent.* He shook his head in bemusement as she blushed hotly at some of what he revealed.

Savanna chuckled shyly into Oran's amused face. " So you're telling me that my hurting you gives you pleasure and you get off on it?"

Oran laughed heartily down at her. " A bit crude, but yes."

" So if I do this." Was the only warning he got as she pulled his beard hard with both hands bringing his lips to hers with a moaning sigh of need as her arousal narrowed her eyes.

His arousal was instant. Heat filled his blood as he shivered from the mingling of pain and pleasure. She groaned as his member swelled within her trembling body as he gently rocked within her. It didn't take her long to explode into ecstasy her body gripping him tightly with each spasm that shook her to her core. His growl filled the chamber as he felt her nails find his buttocks and dig into his hard flesh as she drove her hips up hard to meet his thrusts. Blood boiling he pulled out and as she cried out in shocked disappointment he flipped her over onto her knees and gripped her quivering hips to sink once more into her.

Savanna was shocked when he pulled out of her and had wondered if she had gone to far when he suddenly flipped her over with a deep growl only to grip her hips with his strong hands and enter her from behind. She gasped in shock at his entry. Her body exploded anew as her orgasm swept through every nerve in her body. His hand found her braid and gripped it hard sending pain and pleasure swirling and in shock felt a burning heat like she had never felt before grip her belly. Tighter he pulled her braid as harder he thrust sending that heat burning hotter and hotter.

" This is what you do to me." He growled dangerously into her ear his breath burning deliciously on her flesh. " Every time you pull my beard or rake your nails over my flesh."

Savanna could only whimper as his words spoke volumes to her dazed mind. She had felt his heat and arousal but to experience it for her-self was another thing entirely. Her whimpers grew as the burning swelled inside her making her quiver like a taut bowstring. His hips held her in place unmoving almost making her sob with her burning need.

" I can hold you like this for hours." He threatened as he then ran his tongue over the back of her neck making her whimper and sob as the burning heightened but didn't let go. " In this way I control when you get pleasure."

The tightness and burning in her belly grew and grew. She was unaware that her nails were digging into the stone under her.

" This is how males punish their females." Again his tongue swept over her over heated flesh tasting the sweat that had broken out all over her. " Or give them a taste of what they do to them. When I make you go over in this position you will experience all the pain and pleasure that I go through every time you pull my beard and draw my blood."

The burning was starting to hurt. The ache grew sharper and sharper. Her breath came in harsh gasps as she burned with pain. His member started to widen inside her. She gasped as her flesh started to stretch from that swelling. Fearing he would rip her open she chocked. " Oran!"

Oran's mouth found her ear and gently sucked sending her crying and gasping as the pain swelled even as he swelled even more within her. She tried to move her hips but he held her motionless with his body. His chuckle sent waves of burning pain through every nerve ending.

" Feel me fill every inch of you." Oran whispered harshly into her ear. " Soon I will not be able to move in you for I will be stuck. We will be stuck until my seed fills every crevice of your body."

Savanna shook. Her eyes wide and staring as he swelled swiftly as he had told her he would. Then he let her go. She felt his triumph fill her.

" Try to escape Savanna." He chuckled softly as his hands ran down her quivering back to her tiny waist. " I dare you to find the solution to your problem. Only pain will bring my seed. Only my seed will free you."

Savanna choked back her sobs as she struggled against him but found her-self truly captured by him. Every movement she made sent her burning pain higher until she could only gasp and quiver uncontrollably. All she had was her hands.

Savanna whimpered as she reached between her legs seeking. Her questing fingers found them locked together. Her flesh stretched tight, his hard and unyielding like hot metal within her. Felt his shiver as her fingers and nails touched him. She tried to scratch his hard flesh but he only chuckled breathlessly at her and he swelled even more. Seeking further she found his hard but yielding sack. With a strangled sob of pain and need she dug her nails into his flesh.

Oran roared as her nails found him. Hot seed rose explosively from deep within him to spasm into her quaking flesh. *I can't leave her like this!*

Savanna felt his seed rising hot within him then felt its molten heat spill into her quivering belly. She sobbed franticly trying to seek her own release but it wouldn't come. Hot tears flowed uncheck down her heated cheeks. *Please don't do this to me*!

As if hearing her thoughts Oran snarled and leaned over her. One hand found her braid and wrapped his fist into it and pulled her head back just as his teeth gently bit into the flesh at the base of her throat. The burning pain within her suddenly exploded into emotions so over whelming she screamed in pure rapture as it consumed her body, mind and soul.

    She was lost within the turmoil of emotions. Their emotions blazed through her as one entity. They rode them together bodies straining in their release. Riding each wave as they crashed together in orgasm after orgasm. Her mind screamed at the overwhelming sensations that shattered through her quivering body. Felt his hips slam into her sending them both spinning even higher. Felt his member pulse within her as it spilled its second load of boiling seed within her. Then they floated back to reality gasping and quivering with the aftershocks that made both of them spasm with remembered pleasure.

    Oran's lips trailed over her still quivering skin sending bumps rising in reaction. He chuckled as he then released her and slowly stood up.

    " Come lets go soak in the hot water." He smiled down at her as he held out his hand.

    Savanna looked speculatively at his hand before taking it with her shaking one. What she had felt this last time felt more than just a roll in the hay, as her twin would have called it. It went deeper.

    Together they slowly entered the hot pool. Their body's touching here touching there. A brush of fingers making flesh shiver in delight soon turned into exploring that once more turned hot and explosive between them.

Garth raised a questioning brow when Braun suddenly scowled and swiftly exited the cave.

Garn chuckled heartily at his departure. Then saw the look on Garth's face and burst out laughing. If his brother couldn't figure it out he wasn't going to be the one to enlighten him.

Braun returned a few hours later looking much calmer than he had when he left. He was followed a few minutes later by Savanna and Oran. They all gathered around the fire for a final cup of tea before calling it a night.

Oran wrapped his arms around Savanna holding her close to his chest. She fell asleep to the beat of his heart as he kissed her brow before closing his eyes to fall into a dreamless sleep.

The following days were much the same except nothing attacked them. They rode out before dawn only stopping at mid-day to eat and rest then ride again till nightfall. The weather stayed remarkably fair until they got to the base of the mountain then the next day snow met their eyes as they exited their tents.

Savanna's skill at riding improved. She was now able to ride without getting exhausted by nightfall. Her muscles still burned but now she liked the feel of the pain, it exhilarated her.

She found her pony a delight to ride even coming to love the trot. Oran had taught her how to care for him and how to put his tack on in the morning and how to take it off at night. Brushing him with his comb she had found soothing to both her and Sunny and their bond grew till Sunny would but his head gently into her as he nibbled her hair almost lovingly as she combed his mane.

It had taken them three weeks to reach the pass that Beldin feared would be blocked by snow. At mid-morn they came around a corner to stop in surprise. The pass was indeed blocked but instead of snow large boulders filled the roadway.

Savanna stared at the boulders as her nausea grew. Her stomach churned and she tasted bile. She hadn't been feeling good since she got up that morning and riding Sunny had made her nausea worse.

Savanna felt it rise and quickly jumped off Sunny and had barely reached the sparse bushes and boulders on the side of the road before her breakfast of bread and tea spewed violently from her mouth.

Oran was instantly at her side holding her steady as she continued to expel everything in her stomach. She chocked and gasped trying to breathe between her retches. Dry heaves shaking her uncontrollably as tears ran down her chilled face.

There was a flurry of activity behind them as Savanna fought control over her body. Shaking and sobbing she leaned into Oran as her legs started to give out.

" I got you." He whispered as he picked her up into his arms and carried her back to the others.

Someone had erected a tent off the road, and the smell of tea brewing filled the cold air as Oran took her inside it. Concern filled faces looked at her when he placed her on the bed already set up to receive her.

" Here eat this." Garn said as he held out a gnarled white root. " See if that helps."

Oran stiffened at the sight of the root that Garn handed to her. His eyes widened as he looked down at Savanna and he wasn't the only one watching with held breath for all eyes were now on her.

Savanna hesitated before taking it. She didn't trust her stomach to keep this strange root down much less the tea that even the smell of was making her stomach roil. Gingerly she wrinkled her nose and then put the root into her mouth. Instantly she started to feel better as the roots juices calmed the roiling within her belly and the woody taste helped clear the horrible taste of vomit from her tongue.

" Feel better?" Garn asked as he looked at her closely.

" Yes." Savanna answered surprise in her shaking voice then held up the root it looked like ginger but the taste was different. " What is this?"

Garn chuckled his eyes full of merriment. " Chava root."

He patted her hand and said. " Gavan gave it to me before we left. He thought you'd need it before you reached the Holt."

Savanna looked at her uncle suspiciously.

" Gavan sent this for me?"

She looked up at Oran who stood staring at her with a bemused smile on his face and the others were grinning hugely down at her. Her eyes narrowed as she sent her gift into her-self to see if she was coming down with the flue and was shocked by what she found.

Savanna stared at her belly in amazement. Her eyes widened as her gift allowed her to see the life that grew within her. Shaken and scared she looked up at Oran as her hand went to touch her still flat belly. " I'm pregnant?"

Oran grinned his eyes beaming at her. " Chava root only works on pregnant females."

Savanna then asked her eyes wide, afraid of his answer. " Do you want children Oran?"

Oran crouched before her with a gentle chuckle. " Yes. I do. The more the merrier."

Savanna grimaced as her stomach growled hungrily within her. "Good because the twins are hungry and I really would like to eat."

CHAPTER FOURTEEN

Savanna watched as Oran's eyes widened then narrowed as her words sank in then was surprised by the hug he proceeded to give her as his body shook. His laughter filled the tent as he pulled back enough to put his large hand over her belly.

" Twins?" Oran looked at her in wonder. Then looked at the others with pride shinning in his face. " Do you hear that. We're going to have twins!"

Garn handed her a cup of tea while Garth shooed everyone from the tent. " Put your exuberance to work by clearing the rock from the road. The sooner it's cleared the sooner we can get to the Holt."

Oran would have stayed but one look from Garth made him change his mind. Kissing her brow warmly he said. " I'll return soon."

Garth and Garn chuckled heartily when he left.

" That lad is going to have his world turned upside down when the twins are born." Garn snickered eyes twinkling as he sat next to Savanna on the bed. " So twins. Guess your wondering what the excitements all about?"

Savanna snickered at the understatement. " That's putting it mildly but yes. Why would my being pregnant make everyone almost giddy? Don't your females get pregnant?"

Garth almost chocked on his tea trying not to laugh as she looked at Garn with a raised brow. He wagged a finger at Garn as his body shook with laughter. Tears of mirth rolling down his cheeks to disappear into his beard.

Garn swatted at his finger amused. " I know. I know. She's a Dwarf. Do you think you can handle this conversation any better?" Garn said as he went to stand up. " I'll leave you to it."

Garth sputtered in horror as Garn headed to the door. " No! No, You can have this one all on your own! I'll just go help the others."

Garn chuckled as the older Dwarf made a hasty retreat out of the tent. He looked at Savanna with a huge smile on his face. " That's the first time he's left me to deal with an important conversation. Usually he has to stay to put his two bits into a teaching session."

Savanna giggled as her uncle waggled his brows at her. Out of all of her uncles she felt closer to him. He always made her laugh or smile. " Is it going to be embarrassing, this lesson you have in mind for me?"

" It depends on what Oran has already touched on about males and females if he even had that conversation with you yet." Garn told her his own cheeks starting to redden even though he still chuckled.

Savanna blushed deeply as she remembered the conversation Oran had with her at the pool. " He told me some though the talk about pregnancy never came up."

Garn chuckled. " Let me guess he got into the finer points of the mating rituals?" then shook his head in annoyance at her nod and at the blush that suffused her face. " Never took into consideration that he might get you pregnant did he?"

" I think we're both at fault there." Savanna whispered as she looked nervously down at her hands clenched in her lap. " I wasn't thinking of pregnancy when we.." she blushed even deeper.

Garn coughed as embarrassed as his niece. " Well needless to say who's to blame I need to teach you about pregnancy for a Dwarf female and the changes we males are going to have around you especially as your belly starts to swell."

Savanna smiled shyly as she nodded her head in understanding. She hoped it wasn't going to be too embarrassing.

" First off the sickness will get worse." He told her as she groaned at his words. " I have three more roots hidden in my packs. They will help. You need to chew on them first thing each morning and any time you feel ill."

Savanna sighed and nodded. So far this conversation wasn't to bad maybe all he was going to tell her was how to keep her food down.

" Second thing is your emotions. They will become stronger the further you go into your pregnancy." Garn blushed deeply and he coughed again then gently took her hands in his and said with seriousness in his voice. " Your need will burn more powerfully. Oran will have to deal with this when they hit. He may have to take you in front of us."

Savanna looked at him horrified. The thought of Oran taking her in front of anyone made her feel ill. ***Gods please don't let that happen***!

Garn patted her hands as he chuckled weekly. " Hopefully we will be in the Holt then and within the helping arms of your female relatives before they hit full force for they are more equipped to handle this situation then us males." Then winked at her. " That is why our females never leave the Holt."

Savanna squeezed his hands. " Lets hope we get to the Holt in time then." She blushed as she looked up into his eyes. " But if we don't." She closed her eyes. " Will you think less of me if he does have to deal with that in front of all of you?"

Garn hugged her to him as he kissed her brow with a chuckle. " That my dear we males have been dealing with for millennia. If that happens we will form an armed ring around the two of you. We will stand guard until your both done."

" Then if it happens it happens as long as no one thinks badly about me over it." Savanna smiled weekly up at him, though she still felt horrified about it.

Garn chuckled. " Want some more tea? And maybe some bread and cheese?"

" Yes I think I should." She giggled as her stomach once more growled. " They are hungry."

" Do you know the sex of them yet?" Garn asked curious.

Savanna thought for a minute then sighed. " No."

Garn brought over the tea and a chunk of cheese and a loaf of bread. He tore chunks from each and handed them to her as he tore chunks for him-self. They ate in silence. Outside they could hear the rumble of rock as the others worked on clearing the road.

" Well now that we covered that." Garn said around a sip of tea. " You need to know about us males."

Savanna chuckled softly. " Is it going to be painful like the last session?"

Garn laughed heartily. " For us males yes. Especially for Braun who is linked to you." Then he chuckled knowingly as his eyes twinkled at her with amusement. " I think you have already experienced one bout of need already. The night when Oran took you to the hot pool."

Savanna closed her eyes as a groan escaped from her throat. " Why would you say that? What happened?"

" Just after you and Oran left Braun got up and left the cave in a hurry." He chuckled. " Two hours later he returned and close on his heals came you and Oran."

Savanna's eyes widened as she put the pieces together. " Oh!"

She blushed in shame and went red with embarrassment. " Is there a way for him to block my emotions so he can't feel them?"

Garn shook his head sadly. " No child he can't. He will have to deal with your emotions in any way he can."

Savanna paled as she finally understood. She knew what he would do to deal with her need. Shaking she looked into Garn's face as her tears fell. **Oh Braun what have I been doing to you?**

Garn let her sob as he gently patted her hands trying to comfort her. His eyes darkened with his own sadness for he understood what she was going through.

Braun entered the tent his eyes going to Savanna worry upon his face his voice almost dangerous. " Why is she crying?"

Savanna looked up at him her eyes filled with sadness and said simply. " I weep for you."

Braun quickly strode to her and knelt in front of her. Gently he took her hands into his instantly knowing why she wept. " I knew what I was getting into the night I took your blood. When it gets too much I will deal with it. You're my half sister and sharing your emotions is the greatest gift siblings can share. Never think that I regret any of this."

He kissed her lightly on her brow. " Now wipe those tears away and give me a hug."

Savanna did as he asked and wiped her tears on her sleeve. Then she leaned into Braun's chest wrapping her arms around his neck as he held her gently to him. he whispered into her hair. " We'll all get through this."

Garn sighed. " I was about to tell her about the males reaction to her pregnancy."

Braun chuckled. " This is one part of it. We'll get very protective of you from this moment on. Any groan, sigh, or tear and we'll be all over you trying to rectify what ever is bothering you." Then with a chuckle he added. " We will also get angry with you if you do anything that upsets us like going into danger. So no more battles for you my girl. We won't let you or your babies come to harm."

" Not to mention going out of our way to satisfy any weird cravings you may get." Garn chuckled at her as she suddenly blushed then snickered at Braun. " Can you see Oran hunting for wild boar at night?"

At the mention of boar meat Savanna's mouth tingled. She hadn't had boar since she had left the village after finding her twin. The memory of boar's juicy flesh made her groan and close her eyes as her hunger for it suddenly intensified.

She looked up at them and said innocently. " Is there boar around here?"

Both Dwarves looked at her in surprise. Then they both laughed as they came to the same conclusion.

" Are you craving boar meat?" Garn suddenly chuckled his eyes dancing.

Savanna grinned. " Yes."

Braun let her go as he stood up with a chuckle. " I'll go see if any of the others want to go hunting.

There are fresh boar tracks about a quarter mile back from here."

Savanna watched him leave the tent with laughing eyes.

Braun walked over to Oran who was helping Beldin and Moag to push a boulder to the side of the road muscles bulging. He waited for them to finish with the boulder before getting their attention with a wave of his hand.

" Anyone interested in hunting boar?" He asked as they strode over to him.

Moag looked questioning into his face and then groaned. " She craving boar?"

Oran and Beldin laughed at the chagrined expression on Moag's face. Their laughter got the attention of the others who curiously joined them. Soon they were all chuckling.

Moag snorted. " Hunt boar or move rocks? Well count me in the hunt. Wouldn't mind some fresh meat for supper getting tired of bread and cheese."

They were all in agreement. The chance to have fresh boar meat made them all smile as they chose who would go and who would stay to guard the tent. Moving rocks now on hold as the hunters took to their ponies and headed back down the road.

Tobin, Beldin and Oran remained behind to watch the camp.

Braun led the others back to where he had seen the tracks. They left the ponies tied to some trees as they set out on foot following the boar through the rocky terrain. The tracks clear in the snow.

The tracks led them to a small pool fed by a small waterfall. Crouching down they waited.

Then it came.

Big and black the boar walked out of the bushes and went to take a drink from the pool. Its razor tusks curled around its mouth. Muscles rippled under its shaggy coat of winter hair.

Braun threw his axe as it swung around for it had smelled them. With a grunt it collapsed with the axe imbedded into its brain. Chuckling Braun went to retrieve his axe from the boar. His hand had just gripped the handle when a squeal behind him made him turn just as the boars mate slammed into him.

Her weight threw him to the ground as she swept her head back and forth trying to slash him with her tusks her squeals of rage filling the air just as the rest of the Dwarves swarmed out of the bushes.

Braun wrapped his thick arms around her shaggy neck and squeezed with all his might. His blood burned with blood lust as he squeezed the life from the female boar. Here was the outlet for all his pent up tension!

The others cheered him on all of them caught up with the struggle. Wagers were set. He controlled his breathing as the boar fought to get free. Then with a growl and a twist her neck broke with an audible snap and she lay still in his trembling arms.

It didn't take them long to gut and skin both animals. Leaving the guts on the ground they tied the carcasses to two poles and headed back to camp.

Braun grinned for his tension was gone.

Fear! Rage! Pain! Blasted threw him making him stumble to his knees in shock. He roared in anguish. " Savanna!!!"

Garn walked with Savanna out of the tent. She needed to relieve her-self and he showed her where the makeshift latrine was. He turned around so she would have privacy while she used the trench that had been dug for that purpose.

His eyes scanned the rocks and trees for movement. Pain exploded in his head and he watched in amazement as the ground came up to meet him. Savanna screamed then he knew nothing more as darkness took him.

Oran found Garn. The old dwarf lay unconscious on the ground with blood covering his face. Savanna was nowhere to be seen. Signs of a struggled spoke volumes as to what had happened to her. Someone or something had taken her. Her dagger lay on the ground half buried in the snow.

Oran stared into the wilderness and shook. She was out there defenseless in danger!

Oran threw back his head and roared his rage and fear and grief to the sky. " Savanna!"

CHAPTER FIFTEEN

Savanna struggled against the ropes that bound her. The filthy cloth in her mouth made her gag but she controlled her-self from vomiting. Terror filled her as she watched the one who had grabbed her build a fire in the cave he had taken her to. She shook uncontrollably in fear. ***Is he going to kill me!?***

She had screamed when he had struck Garn on the head with his club. Her heart had frozen in shock as Garn fell unmoving to the ground. In fear she had drawn her dagger and attacked but he was too fast and had disarmed her. He had grabbed her and hit her in the face with his fist. Dazed she was defenseless as he bound and gagged her then had swung her over his shoulder to run fast into the wilderness at times almost flying. So fast did they travel that the ground blurred in her vision making her black out. She had awakened to find her-self sitting against stone.

She studied her abductor with sharp eyes. He was taller than most humans and was extremely thin almost bony. His face was hidden within his cloak so she didn't know what he looked like but his hands were long and heavily veined. Why her alarm system hadn't warned her of him mystified her even now her alarm stayed silent though her mind screamed for her to run.

The fire blazed filling the cave with heat. It cast shadows over the stone around them. He whispered into the fire and the flames swirled and turned a sickly green then he growled. " Ragnok!"

" Ashka Tarn!" A gravely voice hissed from the fire. " Did you find her?"

" Yes, Lord Ragnok." He answered in a deep chuckle like his voice came from the bottom of a well. " She is here."

" Good." The voice from the flame chuckled. " Bring her so I can see her."

Her abductor got up and went to her. She cringed as his hands touched her arm and painfully hauled her to her feet and dragged her to the fire to look upon a dark face wreathed in green flame.

" Ahh. Child you have grown since last we saw each other." The face in the fire giggled at her. " Oh you don't remember? No matter. You were three then and your pitiful mother didn't know what she had birthed."

The fire gurgled with laughter. Her blood started to freeze from the sound and she shivered with cold even though she stood next to the roaring flames.

" What is that on her flesh!" the fire growled in surprised anger. " Who drew on your delicious flesh girl!? Did you do this to her?!" the voice turned on her abductor in rage.

" No!" The hooded one whimpered in fear cowering. " They were already there when I took her from the Dwarves."

The flames crackled and snapped angrily with rage. " Dwarves! You took her from Dwarves!"

The flames hissed and sputtered agitated, as the

face grew ugly in rage. " Fool!"

The fire roared hitting the roof of the cave. " Sorry child but I can't let the Dwarves have you. Interesting as you are. I will have to send your grandfather my condolences but he will understand. I will not have Dwarves seeking me out at this time. Good by child and farewell. Kill her!" then it was gone. The fire went to normal leaving Savanna shaken.

The hooded one gurgled gleefully as he turned to her. " Your brother was easy to kill. His death was so sweet. Will your death match his? Will your soul be as sweet?"

He moved towards her. " I hunger to feed upon your life force child."

He raised his hand at her and she knew that if he touched her she would die! Instantly her alarms went off! *He killed my twin!*

Her blood froze and burned within her. Fire and ice burned as one within her. She would die this night! Her babies would die with her! *I never got the chance to tell Oran I loved him!*

No! Fear! Anger! Grief! RAGE!!

White fire burst from her skin consuming everything on her! Her bonds and clothes gone. The flames swirled with her rage as she stood naked before the hooded one in defiance.

The hooded one screamed in fear as the flames swirled from her to him and his scream turned to pain as her fire consumed him. His shrieks rang shrilly as he burned flapping his arms trying to put them out. The smell of burning flesh filled the cave. With one last shriek he toppled over silent among the flames.

Her flame shot out of the caves mouth shooting into the sky for all to see. Then as suddenly as they had come they were gone. Curling into her flesh to once more become silver runes that moved under her skin for they were now awake and alive sending molten heat through her naked body.

Savanna ran from the cave. She needed Oran. She needed Oran now! Heat burned her inside and out. She stopped looking around almost sobbing trying to figure out how to get back to him. *Where are you Oran? Which way do I go? Right or left?*

Anger and fear leading her to take the left as his emotions slammed into her full force. And the words Braun had told her came back to her *You will always know where he is at all times and what he is feeling...*

Down the path she ran.

Savanna followed the emotions like a compass. Her bare feet hardly touching the ground as she ran following those emotions like a hound after prey.

Braun found Oran on his knees weeping, holding Savanna's dagger to his chest. He stood a few feet from him even though he to wanted to voice his anguish to the sky after Garn had told him what happened. Who ever had taken her had left no tracks for them to follow.

The others stood behind him ready to do battle. Only Garth would remain behind tending to Garn's wounds until they returned.

" She's still alive. We need to go after her before who ever took her harms her." Braun told him hoarsely. " I am your compass to finding her. Use me!"

Oran swung around to look up at him his teeth bared. " They will die for touching her! We will hunt them down and kill every single one that took her from me!"

The nine Dwarves rushed into the wilderness following the one linked to the girl as he led them on her trail.

Savanna stumbled and hit the ground hard snow swirled around her, pain making her cry out as a rock sliced her palm. Bushes had scratched her body leaving bloody runnels down her flesh even as her wounds healed. Her body burned from both pain and need.

Sobbing she climbed to her feet. Her feet burning as she ran over the snow-covered ground. She could feel Oran. He was close.

Two hours later the Dwarves stopped just out side a clearing as white fire blasted into the sky. It formed the Dwarf ring for a few breathes then it was gone leaving the night once more in darkness.

" Wait!" Braun hissed.

Eyes closed he took in Savanna's emotions as they swirled through him. " She comes! We will wait here!"

Oran turned to look at him with rage filled eyes. " Lead me to her!"

Braun stood staring at the other side of the clearing. " Wait!"

Oran gripped his axe and was about to snarl.

" Every one step into the clearing!" Braun hissed.

As one they all stepped into the clearing passing Oran the moonlight bathing them in its light. Oran growled and stepped past them.

A call from the other side of the clearing caught their attention and out of the bushes ran Savanna. Her naked rune marked body glowed in the moonlight.

Savanna found the stream literally as she fell gasping into its chilled waters. Chocking and sputtering she waded through the current to the other side. Shaking with cold she climbed onto the bank. Her need to find Oran giving her strength as she continued through the forest of snow covered trees.

His emotions a blinding beacon in her mind. Telling her that he was near. Her feet found a sheet of ice and she came down hard at the edge of a clearing.

Gasping for breath for her wind had been knocked from her she looked up just as nine figures stepped out of the forest on the other side. They stood bathed in moonlight.

Her eyes widened with unshed tears as she recognized them. Then Oran moved to the front and looked right at her.

Oran!

Savanna found her-self on her feet running to him.

"Oran!" she screamed as she ran to him and flung her-self into his arms weeping.

Oran caught her up in his strong arms and held her tightly to his shaking chest as he kissed her. His mouth was hot and almost savage on hers. Heat blasted through her blood.

Oran went to let her go but her sudden growl and gripping hands held him to her. Her nails ripped at his armor seeking his flesh. Metal fell away with ease as her hands touched it.

"Dwarven ring now!" Braun commanded his eyes blazing. "Oran! Join with her now!"

Oran didn't need the hint for he was already pulling the rest of his Armor off to let it fall into the snow.

His blood on fire and was already blazing in his eyes as Savanna pulled his hair in her need. Savanna felt the heat of his flesh. Whimpers rose deep from within her as she felt him tug his breaches off to stand naked before her. His hard body crushing her to him as molten heat shared blazed through her boiling blood.

Oran lifted her and his huge member found her opening sliding deep into her moist boiling core. Her legs gripped his waist as she rode him savagely as the eight Dwarves formed their ring around them their faces hard and eyes blazing. Then they faced outwards weapons in hand and ready for battle as their eyes watched the forest.

Braun boiled as he was linked to the girl in the center of the ring. Her cries of need filling his ears and mind even as they filled the night around them. His pain intensified until he was gasping with it.

" Deal with your pain lad!" Beldin growled next to him. " Before your lust destroys you!"

Braun growled almost savage him-self as he obeyed his uncle. His hand found his member hard and throbbing. Gripping him-self with hard fingers he fought for his own release as the pair in the center savagely mated. Then it blazed through him, her orgasm was powerful, sweeping through him making his head blaze as his seed exploded onto the ground.

Savanna was unaware of what she was doing to Braun. Her body shook with her orgasm. Then it rose again more powerful then the first shaking her to her very soul. In ecstasy she threw back her head and screamed as another claimed her and another. Her nails raked Oran's back drawing blood and his own orgasm as his seed spilled into her. His roar drowning out her scream of pleasure. Waves rippling through them both as their bodies shook from the aftermath.

Braun shook in shock. His seed had spilled almost endlessly from him with each orgasm Savanna had. Beldin held him from falling as he shook and quivered. He had almost blacked out from them and sparks still danced over his vision. Gasping he slowly released his now shrinking member though aftershocks from her still swept through him.

" We need to find you a wife lad." Beldin growled gently as he held his nephews shaking body. " Or send you to another Holt far from her."

Braun glared up at his uncle. " Find me a wife! I'm not leaving her!"

The Dwarves waited for them to dress though for Savanna a cloak had been provided to cover her nakedness. Oran then picked her up once he was dressed in his armor though Tobin was carrying his chain mail for the girl had made it into a sheet.

Savanna leaned into his chest wrapping her fingers gently into his warm beard with a sigh of contentment. " Sorry about the chain mail. I wanted to feel your skin so bad and it just happened."

Hearty chuckles from the males answered her words.

Oran kissed her brow as he chuckled warmly against her. His breath was warm and soothing on her skin. Exhaustion swept over her as they headed back to the camp. Her eyes closed and sleep took her.

Savanna woke to the smell of roasting boar. Her stomach growled as her hunger made it-self known. She opened her eyes to find her-self still against Oran's chest.

"We're almost to the camp." He told her as he chuckled. " Garn and Garth must have gotten the boar cooking while we were gone."

" Good cause I'm hungry." Savanna sighed as her stomach growled again. She grimaced as hunger burned painfully within her. Then she remembered Garn falling and guilt filled her. ***Here I am thinking of my-self and Garn could be seriously injured!***

" Garn?" Savanna trembled as she looked up at Oran.

" He's fine." Braun came to walk next to them. " He was more angry then hurt when we left to find you."

Braun looked at her. " He blames him-self for letting you get taken."

Savanna pursed her lips then shuddered. " Then he's a fool! That thing that took me could have killed him with a single touch."

Oran stopped to look down at her his eyes wide. " With a touch?"

Savannas nodded her eyes filled with grief and unshed tears. " He was the one who killed my twin."

CHAPTER SIXTEEN

Savanna sat staring into the flames of the large fire that Garn and Garth had made to cook the boars over. She was once more fully clothed but still felt naked as she remembered Oran taking her in the clearing with all the others watching.

That bothered her more than she wanted to admit to either Oran or Braun who sat on either side of her. Grief over her twin was also raw within her making her sorrow even worse.

Garn came to stand over her his eyes filled with the guilt that Braun spoke of.

Savanna stood up and with a sob hugged him. She felt him shudder then he wrapped his arms around her. All she could do was cry into his beard.

The crackling of the fire and her sobs filled the night for every one was silent. No one spoke as they grimly watched her cry.

Garn kissed her brow as his tears flowed down his cheeks and into her hair. " Forgive me lass. I should have been more vigilant."

" It's not your fault." Savanna sniffed looking up at him. " Your lucky he only hit you with that club. If he had touched you he would have eaten your life force."

" That's the second time you mentioned his killing with a touch." Oran came to stand next to them his eyes thoughtful. " Now you mention he eats peoples life forces as well. Was he tall, say taller than a human."

Savanna nodded her eyes wide in fear.

Garn stiffened as his arms tightened around her as growls from the rest suddenly burst around them.

" Vulsgard!" Braun hissed hand on his axe his eyes gleaming as he also came to stand next to them. " Did he have a name?"

" Ashka Tarn." Savanna told them. " That is what the face in the flames called him."

Oran growled and he wasn't the only one to do so. All eyes were now on her and Garn pulled her back so he could look into her face. The looks they gave her made her shudder in fright.

" What did the face in the flames look like." Garn asked her his voice gentle but his eyes burned dangerously into hers.

Savanna told them as best she could as she shook in terror for their emotions were consuming her, freezing her blood. " Couldn't see it very well. His face looked like it was melted and the one who took me called him, Lord Ragnok."

" Ragnok!" Moag snarled.

" He's dead!" Oran growled dangerously hand on his axe as he glared at Moag. " My uncle died when he tried to steel my fathers throne."

Savanna sobbed and shook from the emotions as their rage and hate filled her and she begged. " Please no more."

Garn pulled her against him as she shook and sobbed uncontrollably clinging to him. He looked at

Oran and said. " Control your emotions! All of you! She's almost like ice!"

Suddenly the emotions of rage and hate that had been swelling inside her were gone replaced by feelings of guilt and concern. Shuddering she wept softly as Oran gently took her from Garn and pulled her against him his lips kissing her upturned face. Kissing the trail of her tears sending warmth through the block of ice her body had become.

" Sorry lass." Garn whispered as he gently patted her shoulder trying to send reassurance to her. " We needed to know who took you and why."

Savanna shook as she told them everything. " He never said why he had me taken. He wasn't happy that I was with Dwarves and he didn't like the runes on my skin. Before he left he told me he would send his condolences to my grandfather then he told the one who had taken me to kill me then he was gone leaving me alone with the hooded one."

Savanna buried her face into Oran's beard. "He started to reach for me and I got scared and angry. He had killed my twin! He was going to keep me from you! He was going to kill our babies!"

Oran shook as he held her tightly kissing her face and whispering soothingly into her ear then asked. " What was the light that lit up the night sky?"

Sobbing Savanna looked up at him with haunted eyes. " My runes came to life! They turned into flames and swirled around me then they hit him and he burst into flame! They consumed him and then exploded into the night sky! Once he was dead they came back to me. They burned Oran! All I could think of was getting to you."

" So that's what happened to your clothes." Braun sighed his voice harsh from all her emotions. " The runes consumed them."

" So you killed a Vulsgard." Garth chuckled as he pulled some meat from one of the boars and started to heap a plate with it. " Oran sit with her before the poor child collapses."

Oran growled and glared at him but didn't argue as he sat down pulling Savanna into his lap. Savanna had once again claimed his beard with both hands.

Oran sat deep in thought worry lined his face. *If Ragnok still lives my father and our entire Holt will be in danger.* He kissed Savannas brow as his need to protect her made him shudder at how close she had come to dying. *For a Vulsgard to obey his commands means he's aligned him-self with the mages.* Dread filled him. *The mages have access to our secrets.*

" You're going to have to let him go sometime." Braun chuckled as he sat next to them. " Besides it's pretty hard to eat boar meat with you hands tangled in his beard."

Savanna giggled through her tears at his words. Reluctantly she let go of Oran's beard with a groan as Garth handed her a plate loaded with hot boar's meat. Hungrily she tore into it with her teeth. The juice ran down her chin but she didn't care her hunger was too urgent a need to ignore any more.

" It seems you have defenses that will kick in when you're defenseless." Garn sighed as he crouched in front of her. " The Gods are protecting you. The answers might be in these runes. Until we get you to the Holt we are going to have to stay close to you at all times."

Savanna looked up at him her hunger now under control. She was now feeling almost normal. " I think I might need to make my-self clothes that won't get consumed by the runes. Ending up naked every time they burn isn't fun."

They all looked at her runes in contemplation.

" The only materials I can think of that our runes don't destroy are precious stones and metal." Beldin chuckled as he put a piece of meat into his mouth. " Now the first won't change their form for any gift but metal can."

Savanna licked the juice from her fingers as she contemplated his words. She went over every metal she could think of. The only thing that would be light enough for her to wear would be silver mixed with steel like her dagger only it would have to be thin like silk. An image of the veils worn by Oran's mother in his dream/memory surfaced. Her mind worked with the idea. His mother had been completely covered in veils but that wouldn't work for her. She needed to have a clear path to her dagger if she ever got in trouble. The idea to cover her runes with veils was appealing and knew that Oran would like her in veils made her smile.

Braun chuckled softly next to her. " You feel like the cat who stole the cream."

Savanna smile secretively at him but said nothing as her mind formed her outfit. She looked over at her uncle Garth and asked innocently. " Would you help me in making my outfit?"

Garth almost chocked on his meat. Sputtering he took a drink of tea before looking sharply at her from across the flames. " It's my gift you're asking the use of is it?"

Savanna smiled at him batting her eyes coyly at him. " Why uncle what ever gave you that idea?"

The others roared in laughter while Garth raised a brow at her. He mumbled something about the cheekiness of females that set them all roaring with laughter again.

" Besides you left poor uncle Garn to fill me in on the details of being pregnant." Savanna grinned wickedly at him eyes sparkling with humor. " The least you can do is help me make a simple outfit."

Garn chortled at the look of disgruntlement that filled Garths face at her words. Eliciting another roar of laughter from the others as he wagged a finger at his brother. " That'll teach you for running out on her."

Garth glared at him. " You're not being very helpful."

Oran laughed so hard tears were running down

his face into his beard. He held his mate closer to him. This was the outlet they all needed the laughter released all the pent up tension every one was still feeling since finding her and learning that Ragnok still lived.

    Savanna basked in the gentle warmth of their laughter. Her eyes danced with mirth as she then gave her uncle some false ideas just to get a reaction from him to keep the laughter going.

    Braun doubled over roaring. He could feel what she was doing and approved whole heartily as she baited the old Dwarf.

    Garth sputtered and growled indignantly at each idea she threw at him. He saw her game and found playing his part pure delight as she tried to bait him with each outfit more outlandish than the last until he finally growled. " Ok I'll help you with your outfit." He wagged a finger at her as he said. " But I decide on what it looks like. I would hate to see the outfit if I left it all in your hands."

    Savanna grinned in triumph for she had won this battle. " Agreed."

    The banter continued around the fire. They talked and laughed as they all ate the boar meat until Savanna yawned then with a chuckle Oran took her to the tent.

    Inside was only one bedroll. The one she had been resting on.

    She raised a questioning brow at Oran. " Where's everyone else going to sleep?"

"Outside." He told her with a chuckle. "They are going to guard us while we sleep."

"Oh." Savanna blushed as she looked again at the bedroll. Suddenly she felt shy as she remembered her actions in the clearing. "Just sleep?"

Oran chuckled and pulled her against his chest with a kiss to her brow then kissed her cheek then found her neck making her gasp and shiver with reaction. He shed his clothing even as she shed hers, eyes bright with arousal. They slowly sank to the bedroll kissing and touching as their blood burned.

Savanna gasped as they joined in gentleness. His body was one with hers. Then the gentleness turned harder as their arousal grew. Both straining and gasping as their pleasure grew within them. *I love this male!*

"Do you feel my heat?" Oran growled into her ear as his teeth nipped her lobe. "You took my blood that first time I was on you. Do you remember my grinding into you as I held you down?"

Savanna shook as she remembered and breathed. "I feel you Oran. I feel you all the time."

Oran thrust his hips hard into her then slowly pulled out then thrust hard again into her depths. "Tell me what you feel Savanna? I need to know what I make you feel when I do this."

"Ahh, Oran." Savanna moaned as her pleasure and his rose within her. "I feel your pleasure and mine they swirl as one within me. Your heat burns with mine. Your arousal heightens mine making me want to rip my nails into your flesh."

Savanna ran her nails down his back to dig them gently into his buttocks as they once more thrust into her making her head swim with pleasure. " Yes! Like that! Oh! Oran!"

Savanna exploded in a shower of sparks and ecstasy as her orgasm shook her but some how it wasn't enough she ached for something but didn't know what it was.

" I feel your orgasm Savanna." Oran groaned as he took her mouth with his. " I feel the tremors squeezing me deep within your hot depths. Your heat calling for my hot seed to spill into your quivering body."

Savanna arched into him as once more she exploded with intense pleasure as her orgasm took her again and again as his words and emotions roared through her but she wanted more!

" Rake me with your nails!" Oran growled savagely as he pounded into her fast and hard.

She could feel his need burning within him. Felt his pain rising to join his pleasure. She held back wanting to see how far his pain and need would take them both as if hungry for it.

Oran sensed her hesitation and knew what she wanted and he shook as his pain rose. He gritted his teeth in realization. " Savanna! This is dangerous ground you tread. You need to rake me with your nails!"

Savanna growled deep within her as his pain suddenly consumed her own pleasure. It hurt! It burned her very flesh! This is what she had been craving!

Oran roared as blood lust consumed him!

Savanna saw red and she was filled with blood lust both his and hers joining as one within her! Pain as his teeth bit savagely into her shoulder as she raked her nails viciously into his back! They battled together as their blood lust raged!

He held her pinned to the bedroll as he savagely slammed into her. His seed exploding in a shower of molten pain that shook him to his very soul and he arched back and his roar filled the tent as his seed spilled into her belly.

Savanna exploded in pain both his and hers! She felt his seed spill molten within her as she too screamed! Fire blazed along her skin as her runes came alive. They flowed from her to him bathing him in their flames. Together they burned in white fire!

Oran collapsed upon her trembling in shock. He tasted blood and knew he had bitten her. Into his mind swirled her memories and he felt her emotions. Felt her satisfaction filling her as well as exhaustion. Felt her love for him.

" I feel you Savanna." Oran told her trembling. " I feel your love for me."

Savanna held him to her quivering body. She didn't want to let him go. Closing her eyes she let her emotions lose so he could feel all of her hiding nothing from him she bared her very soul to him.

" Savanna!" Oran chocked as her emotions swirled through him. Tears rolled down his face as he pulled back to look down at the tiny female beneath him with wonderment in his eyes.

" This is how you make me feel." Savanna smiled lovingly up at him. " Yes Oran I do love you."

Oran kissed her lips tenderly. " I love you Savanna. I almost died in grief when he took you from me."

Savanna smiled up at him then gasped as her fingers trailed over the silver runes marking his neck, shoulders and chest. " Oran! My runes have marked you!"

Savanna watched as Oran stood naked before her admiring eyes. Her hand trailed over the runes that had marked his dark skin in their silvery lines and swirls. They were beautiful.

" Is this how they look on me?" She asked as she walked around to his back. They flowed down his neck over his shoulders and down his back and chest. " They are beautiful."

Oran felt her fingers trailing over his flesh and shivered with pleasure at her touch. Felt her shiver with pleasure as her emotions swirled into him.

" Yes." He chuckled. " They are beautiful."

" What does this mean for us?" She whispered when she once more stood before him. Her eyes were shadowed but he could feel her fear as she looked worriedly up at him.

"I don't know." Oran told her as he pulled her to his chest. Once more her fingers found his beard and gently wrapped them-selves in it. Her pleasure and comfort filled him, as he now knew why she did it and chuckled.

Savanna smiled into his eyes and chuckled throatily laughter filling her eyes. "I wonder what my uncles are going to say about this."

Oran groaned closing his eyes as he kissed her brow. "I'm not looking forward to their comments or their laughter over this."

Savanna giggled as she buried her face into his beard and then her yawn brought a chuckle from him.

"It can wait for the morning." Oran chuckled as he once more lowered her to the bedroll. "You need to sleep."

Savanna laid her head upon his chest. Her hands still gripped his beard as she chuckled. "I must agree with you on that one. There's been too much excitement already. If I know my uncles they would keep us both up trying to figure this out. Mmm and sleep sounds so go right now." Another yawn took her as she blinked. "I love you Oran."

Oran kissed her brow as he chuckled. "I love you too. Now close those lovely eyes and go to sleep."

With a sigh she closed her eyes and fell asleep to the beating of his heart.

Savanna tried not to laugh as her uncles made Oran remove his shirt so they could view his new runes as soon as they left the tent. Her hand covered her quivering lips as tears of mirth rolled silently down her cheeks. When Oran glared at her she lost control and giggled helplessly at him, she could feel his chagrin as he growled. " Don't say it!"

The ' I told you so' she wanted to voice stayed in silence as she doubled over laughing so hard her belly started to ache.

Once satisfied her uncles told him he could dress then looked at her with raised brows. That set her off again, giggling uproariously.

Oran just shook his head as he looked helplessly at Braun. " She's your sister."

Braun grinned at him and said. " So, she's your mate."

Savanna still giggling went to him and gently took his beard in her hands and leaned into his chest as he hugged her with a sigh. The new empathy she now shared with Oran let her send her love down the link they shared only to have him send the same to her as he chuckled.

Braun chuckled and said with a wink. " That's heady stuff you're sharing there."

Savanna let his beard go as her nausea awoke. She pulled the root from the pocket in her cloak and chewed. Instantly it went away to be replaced with a growl as her babies let her know they were hungry. She looked down at them with a gentle smile. **Yes my** *darlings I will feed you. Soon we will be at the Holt and you'll both be safe.*

Savanna shivered as a sense of warning went through her, somewhere ahead, danger was waiting for them.

Oran's hand covered her belly. His eyes looked warmly into hers then said. " We will face what ever comes together. I love you Savanna and I will keep you and our babies safe."

With a sigh she once more buried her hands into his beard and gently pulled him down for a heated kiss. *Yes my love. We are both rune bound now and we will face the future together.*